The
Many Voices
Of
Ryne S. Torres

As Edited By

M J Sewall

A Collection Of His
Short Stories and Poems

Song for Jan by Ryne S. Torres and Larry F. Tomlinson.

Sewall Publishing
P.O. Box 246
Lompoc, Ca. 93438
mjassumption@gmail.com

ISBN-13: 978-1483968797
ISBN -10: 1483968790

First Edition April 2013

ACKNOWLEDGEMENTS

Thank you Rose Torres for saving Ryne's words.
I know you inspired many of them.
I hope they shine through to you.

Thank you, Michele Casteel for all of your help.
The extra set of eyes and the loan of your talents
was invaluable.

Ryne, your contribution to our lives is sorely missed,
but thank God your words live on forever...

EDITOR'S NOTE

- Some selections have been previously published in Ustani Magazine.

- The story *Lost Influence*: The text and the panel characters' names are Ryne's words from science fiction stories he wrote. The panelists' dialogue was contributed by the editor.

- Poems: Many poems and songs were fully completed. Some were constructs using Ryne's phrases with very few changes. Ryne experimented with all Poetic styles and forms. Each poem follows different "rules" of punctuation and structure. Ryne definitely believed in poetic license. So does the editor.

INTRODUCTION

So who the hell is Ryne S. Torres and why should you read anything he wrote? Because he was a great writer. This book is the proof.

Ryne Scott Paul Torres was an Actor, Writer, Musician, Man of Letters and mostly out of work. I write this because he was my friend and that is what he had printed on his business card. Ryne was born in 1960 in Zaragoza, Spain. His father was stationed at the U.S. Air Force base there. He came back to the U.S. as an infant and grew up on the central coast of California.

Ryne was writing since at least age twelve. The earliest *dated* writing is from 1973. He was a great actor working mostly on the stage, but also did many film projects. He studied film and worked in the industry beginning just after high school. He worked mainly behind the camera as a Director. Ryne worked in television as the Director of live news telecasts along with a rich life working in many different fields.

Mostly, he wrote. He leaves behind many great tales, working in many different genres. Life, death, love, loss, first person, third person omniscient, and poetry in every form and on every subject.

The book is in three sections. Short stories, poems and songs, and early writings. The first two are self explanatory. The early writings section is a collection of poems and short stories he wrote before college. I have included them because they're either kind of cool or interesting, or both. They also give some insight into the man, with a clever phrase or good plot twist to boot.

In editing his work, I understood - and the reader must understand, that he was a better writer than me. As a writer myself, with the preconceived notion that I am brilliant... this is a big thing to admit. But I cannot quite turn a phrase like Ryne could. And my attempts at poetry are unfit to print. Believe me.

So, who the hell am I to edit his stuff? Long after his death in 2004, his widow Rose found them and gave me his writings to look through. I simply fell in love with his words. Examining the many rough drafts and the finished products, I learned the language of his writing. Not just where he was going with a story, but the perfectly phrased way he got there.

My job as editor was not to "fix" anything he wrote. I am simply helping the words be what he intended them to be. I have been honored to help Ryne get his words to the world.

There is a lot of very personal stuff here. Many new romances and loves lost. None of it is from a journal, but some of it feels like it is.

To paraphrase a famous author: "not every word is a gem. Every writer has drawers stuffed with unclassifiable scraps of unfinished thought and un-publishable nonsense. That is how it is done. A writer writes constantly and reads a million words by other writers. He has to be a glutton for words, to taste them, to roll in them."

Ryne definitely rolled in them.

I hope you enjoy your journey as much as I did.

The only thing I was worry about is that Ryne might be mad at me for organizing his stuff.

I hope you forgive me buddy.

-M J Sewall, January 2013.

CONTENTS

SHORT STORIES

POEMS & SONGS

EARLY WRITINGS

His life was gentle, and the elements
So mix'd in him that Nature might stand up
And say to all the world, "This was a man!"

~ Julius Caesar, Act V Sc. V

O call back yesterday, bid time return...

~ The Life and Death of Richard
the Second, Act III Sc. II

CENTERING IN

Tom climbed out of the jeep parked on the dune and looked around.

The ocean lay before him in all its vastness. He could feel the tug of cool wind coming off the water. It smelled of salt and seaweed, perhaps even a little stench of death.

As he walked towards the water's edge, he took in everything around him. The sand he walked on was soft and gave way to tiny spurts of grass. To his left the beach continued on, rising here and there to meet the foggy horizon. Then to the right a large rock extended from land and into the ocean. Foam and mist had drenched it and taken its toll on the rough surface. Beyond the rocky interruption Tom couldn't see anything but sand and crying seagulls.

He sat down on the wet shoreline, and noticed how firm it was beneath him. The water was just able to reach the tips of his white tennis shoes. It was high tide now, the afternoon had gone, and so was he.

Alone on the beach that was so full of sounds, he lay back. The sand worked its way through his hair as another wave crashed. The sound of birds calling faded slowly away until only the wind was left. Then that was gone too.

His eyes were closed, he relaxed and slept.

The next wave caught him. ◆◆◆

A STUDY IN SECRETS

PART 1 : IN THE QUIET HOURS

The suitcase was packed and his coat spread out at the end of the bed.

Already it had the smell of travel about it.

Occasionally the young's man's shadow would fall across it as he was straightening the room with slow meticulous care. Everything would have to be in order before he left early the next morning because he did not know when he was coming back. School was going to be out for a month and Christmas had come and gone with merciless lethargy.

When everything at last had been put in its proper place, he flipped the light switch off and drew back the curtains to reveal the quiet dark of night. The Christmas lights that wreathed themselves around the house in blinking colors, threw an eerie glow on his face.

He was handsome in a quiet, subtle way. Brown eyes set in a full, round, expressive face. He usually dressed in casual attire wanting to blend in and not seek attention. This best described him he thought, "wanting to blend in". His friends thought he was a good conversationalist and was possessed of an excellent humor and mind.

Right now that particular part of his anatomy was in utter turmoil, focused on one person, on one thought.

Will she come with me?

He let out a heavy sigh, sat down at his large oaken desk and looked towards the stars. They sparkled and shone brightly as the night wore on, some obscured by chance fingers of fog, some cool and aloof in their splendor.

He heard a knock a few minutes later and turned around to discover his brother's head poking through the partially opened door.

"I'm going to bed now."

"Alright Anthony," he said, wondering when his brother's voice had begun to deepen with maturity.

"Do you want to drive the first leg tomorrow?"

"Sure," he said rising from the chair and beginning to stretch, "you go get some sleep."

Anthony began to leave, shutting the door behind him, but stopped abruptly.

"Has she called?" he inquired softly.

The young man stopped and turned toward the window again.

"No... what time is it?"

"A little after ten."

"Okay. I'll see you in the morning."

Ten o'clock.

She didn't want to go... did she?

It had been a random suggestion, asking her to go east with him to see his sister. He had mentioned it in a 'sentimental flight of fancy' thinking she would never take him seriously.

Now here he was waiting for some kind of confirmation.

"By eleven o'clock," she had said last night. It was almost that time now, and seeing that she hadn't called all day, he felt his faith in love and humanity slowly ebbing away. She had said it last night with all the firmness of honest intent, in her breathless, excited voice.

Yet it was all he could do to stop thinking of her in all her softness and warmth on that cold blustery evening only one night before. And as he thought of this, his smile faded but did not completely go away.

He picked up the picture he kept of her on his desk and held it up to the bright lights from outside. While he stood there smiling at her simple beauty, he noticed a stack of receipts from the florist that he'd been saving. There lay a unique yet precise chronicle of his life during that time. First the red roses he had given her on her birthday, then the yellow ones, then the daisies, more roses, carnations....

PART 2 - HAPPY

Almost two years earlier.

His sophomore year in high school was well on its way to becoming the worst of any he had suffered up to that point.

Then she appeared on campus, transferring from some mysterious private school back east in late January. Like she had always been there. Bright and fresh as the promises of the new year itself, she was full of innovations and exceptionally strong opinions. He liked the idea that some were taken aback by her honesty and openness; the qualities that he was immediately attracted to.

"Who is that?" someone asked from the back row.

She had just finished her first impromptu sketch in drama and bounced off stage with a young girl's self confidence.

"I don't know, but whoever she is, she sure the hell is *somebody*." I replied.

"Amen, brother."

The voices of his friends faded away as he took in all of her.

Her strawberry blonde hair fell to her shoulders and made a perfect frame for her porcelain features. Blue eyes that held onto you whenever she talked and a smile that was at once mischievous and innocent.

He liked her, in a purely... professional attitude, of course.

She had a good sense of blocking, excellent diction and someone had evidently given her acting lessons. She would be an extremely stimulating person to work with.

He decided he was in love with her.

They remained friends, but he never got used to the idea of "just friends". She always seemed to be floating on the outer edge of his small circle of friends, never quite within reach.

One spring day, he decided to say 'to hell with the world' and ask her out. Knowing full well what the situation was, his friends told him he was crazy. He knew that they were right and tried not to get involved with her.

He lasted four days. He called her.

He began, "Hello, I've got some studying to do for a history final and I thought maybe we could go to the library. What do you think?"

"One minute," she replied.

She left the phone and walked into the kitchen where her father sat reading the evening paper.

"Dad, I've got to go to the library to study. I promise we won't be late and I've done the dishes, so..."

"That's fine dear," he said, one eye peering from behind the sports page.

"It's okay," she said back on the phone, "I'll be there in ten minutes."

She grabbed her books and flew out the door in her graceful breezy style. He was there in five, but she didn't notice.

Walking up to the library, she let out a soft moan of mock disappointment.

"The library is closed on Saturday nights now," she said.

"Oh, damn it," he said with the most serious 'I forgot' expression look he could muster.

She broke into a smile and in the soft light of the street lamp she looked more beautiful then he could remember.

"What shall we do instead?" she wondered aloud.

Dinner, and all the walking and talking that followed, was long and luxurious that night. By the time they arrived at her back porch it was one in the morning.

"Will you be in trouble?" he asked.

"No."

She put her arms around his neck and drew him closer to the warmth of her body.

"I love you," he said.

She put a finger to his lips.

"You can't say that," she insisted.

"Why?" he said as he kissed her hand and put it back around his neck.

"You know why," was all she said.

He did know, but did not want to, at least not now. He kissed her again and again, each one keeping that warm, wonderful feeling alive, feeling her supple body against his.

He began to nibble her ear.

"I've got to go," she said.

"Now?" he said and looked at her.

"Yes. Wait for me until I get inside."

Unlocking the door, she quickly turned on the kitchen light. The blaze of the porch light shone on her as she turned around and blew him a kiss.

"Tootles," she said slowly and was gone.

"Tootles." Tootles? he wondered softly, with a smile, breathing in deeply as if to gobble up whatever remained of her in the very air around him. He then wearily closed his eyes, committed the evening to memory and made sure it would stay there, clear and bright, lost in the romantic haze of youthful imagination. He knew that it would eventually be remembered differently and he would not possibly ever feel the same.

Standing in the cool evening air he began to think about belonging, just belonging. As this thought crossed his mind, the smile faded.

It did not, however, completely disappear.

PART 3 - SUMMER ENDS

The two of them had done many silly things before. She had, long ago, accepted her fate and resigned herself to loving the daydreaming adventurer in him, the impassioned lover. The little boy quality of his brown eyes. The afternoons would fall somewhere between the deliberate, slow, steady and lushly romantic poetry he'd written for her, and the time he'd come to pick her up at school dressed as D'artagnan, sword included. It was to her simply another in his long list of dramatic flourishes.

He felt as if he had aged ten years, not just six months. She was somehow different now, or was it he that had changed radically? I know I should let go he told himself, still there was always the kisses, the soft plying of her lips against mine.

Soft, soft, soft.

Holding on and on, she resisted less and less, and sometimes even in the quiet of the evening when everything is still and warm, the chill of the midnight air came into their romance.

The more they tried to figure out all their feelings the more confused it all grew. And after all the false stops and not calling each other... she will never belong to me, he thought.

"We have to decide..."

She stopped him with her eyes. Everything that had been planned so carefully to be said, vanished with her last touch.

PART 4 - REALITY

The headlights from a passing car swung low then exploded onto the front lawn and snapped him back into reality. Now he had returned to the present with all its complex problems.

Somehow it had all changed and perhaps for the better. It did not feel the same as it had that night. She did not talk to him like she used to. It wasn't pure anymore. Yes, they both knew what the proper and sensible thing to do was, they both knew what was right and how it should turn out. Did it make it any less painful?

Was this what they called 'coming to your senses?' If it was, he did not like it. Perhaps it was better this way. At least he would know by tomorrow morning.

The young man went through the house locking doors and turning off lights, pausing only once to hear the peaceful breathing of his sleeping father. He paused from time to time thinking and listening to the sounds of the house.

At last he returned to his own room and fell heavily onto his bed, no longer bathed in warm lights, but now in pitch black. Still fully awake he stared at the dark ceiling, waiting for her call. Well, perhaps he would just rest his eyes, but only for a minute, only for a.....

PART 5 - THE PARTY YESTERDAY

"What am I going to do?" he asked himself. Paul Reynolds stood next to the kitchen door, brushing brown hair out of his eyes, in utter confusion. Why had she looked at him like that? Now he couldn't get Julie out of his mind. Everyone knew how she and Jeff Richards almost seemed to be living together. Tonight though, she had been looking hurt, until Jeff had left in silent fury. Then she was there, sitting across from Paul. Somehow, it wasn't flirting as much as it was an offering.

A minute later Julie Taylor walked into the kitchen with a tray of empty plates and glasses. Her blue-green eyes were hidden beneath long, dark lashes, formed exquisitely in his dreams. Hair fell in reddish-blond cascades to her bare tanned shoulders. The black dress she wore flowed the same way to the floor. She took in everything about her, but it was the perfect face that kept him riveted. Skin, seeming to have been spun of milky crème, fit over high cheek bones. Pouting lips, the same pink ones that had whispered his name so many times, became wet with a sweep of her tongue.

Finally she spoke, the voice sounding like soft wind chimes in a cool breeze.

"Paul, are you okay?"

"Yes," was all he could muster. Fighting the urge to reach out and touch her, he knew what he must do.

"Julie," he said with the finest pronouncement, "plain and simple... I love you."

The smile that broke on her face reinforced his will.

"I know you really love him, and you're tired of hearing this, but..."

"It's all right," she soothed, inching closer. Suddenly she stopped and he felt her lock all those feelings inside again.

"What's the matter Julie?" Paul said, not afraid anymore, "say it..."

She turned her back to him as she headed for the door. Then she felt consoling hands around her waist. She shuddered.

"You're tired of him aren't you? I've seen him hurt you, but it won't happen anymore."

Turning, she was instantly in his arms, looking up with those amazing eyes.

"Stay with me," he whispered, "I'll take care of you."

"Yes, it will be hard with him," she returned with no more volume, "I can handle it though."

They both became silent, each thinking about the penalty for loving someone who they shouldn't.

He had fulfilled the dark romantic dream that had so long been dormant. From the recesses of his mind came that familiar readiness toward loving her. Holding her close that last crazy summer returned with all its broken hearts.

His lips touched hers now, first lightly. Then again, as if to savor a taste lost. Then her slender arms arose and wrapped around his neck. The kiss lasted longer this time.

Why feel so guilty? Was God going to strike him down on the spot? Has he committed such an unforgivable sin because of who he held in his arms?

A door must have opened, because the hint of a cold wind came from the patio. It was a strange wind that blew in, it warned of hardships and trouble. Trouble in the form of his 16 year old, 160 pound best friend and gossip. That would be Mark, he thought.

Mark Hanson walked into the warmed room and found Jeff's girl close to Paul. In fact, they were much too close.

Julie broke his mental process by waltzing by him. Mumbling something about having a good time, she turned the corner and was gone.

Mark's inquisitive, black eyes followed her until she had disappeared.

"What were you doing?" he almost yelled.

Paul walked over to the sink, said nothing and opened a can of soda.

"You're bothering her again. Don't you realize she's forgotten your fling?"

Paul smiled between sips of root beer.

"What are you planning? Are you trying to break them up?" Mark asked.

As he looked at his best friend, with innocent eyes, Paul Reynolds laughed, and put down the can.

"I don't know," was all Paul said.

"She is going to marry him."

"I know," Paul replied, "but she has doubts, she..."

"Everybody is like that... doubts... do you know what people would say...?"

"I don't really care," Paul offered.

Jeff put a hand on his friends shoulder, "you will be sorry, but whatever you do, I will be here when you come back."

"If I come back."

They laughed. Paul Reynolds walked out of the kitchen and into the night.

He found her outside, bathed in the light of a lone street lamp, like out of a film. He took her in, all of her, in one breath as they stood in the cool blue. Her fragrance lingering. He held her tight, snuggled once more and whispered.

"Maybe I can't have you, lady, but when I do find her... wherever she is... she'll be a lot like you."

"Don't ever introduce me, I'll probably hate her."

"We're leaving tomorrow, there's room for one more. No, wait. Sorry, I..." he said.

"No, don't be," she had resigned herself, long ago to her reality, and he was leaving. But for a moment, something in her eyes, something from the past, "I'll... I'll think about it. I will call you by eleven o'clock tomorrow night if..."

"If?" He laughed softly and kissed her goodbye. He squeezed her hand gently but firmly, not wanting to let it go.

She left his embrace and walked back to the house.

'Will I see her again?' he thought to himself, knowing he wouldn't sleep well that night.

PART 6 - LEAVING

The ringing came from far, far away. It grew closer and steadily louder. It was the phone, it had to be... and he could very clearly see the receiver resting in its cradle.

He reached for it...

Anthony switched off the alarm clock and gently nudged his brother awake, "Come on," whispered Anthony, "...come on."

"What time is it?" asked Paul.

"Its six o'clock," replied Anthony.

"She didn't call last night?" asked Paul hopefully.

Anthony looked at his older brother and shook his head, "Get up, we've got to get going."

Anthony helped him up and walked him into the bathroom, turning on the water, "Here, splash some water on your face. You'll feel better."

His brother groggily obeyed, rubbing the sleep from his eyes. Anthony went to pack the car, leaving Paul staring into the mirror. They moved slowly, taking their time to eat a good breakfast and say goodbye to their father.

The mist still clung low to the ground, and was already slowly fading away when they pulled out of the city limits.

Anthony looked at his brother. He stared out at the open gray road stretching forward into the new day. He seemed to find it serene and calming.

"Are you going to be all right?"

"Yes, just fine," offered Paul.

But he felt sorry, stupid and small, all at once. For the next few nights she would haunt his dreams.

PART 7 - TAHOE

Like a purple curtain, slowly unraveled fold by fold, night was descending. It fell in shadows and quiet tunes that darkened with each minute.

The mountainous horizon began coloring in, and then the ceremony was complete, looking even more dormant than before.

It was only when silver stars slid by on a velvet background did the young man stand up from where he had been sitting.

He searched the lake from his vantage point, a small mooring pier, for signs of activity. There were none of any kind.

Miles away though, the lights of south shore sparkled with clarity and a kind of monotonous pattern. They reassured him that humanity still survived somehow, somewhere.

The human mind is a strange thing. At one interval in one's existence it can be completely at ease, while at another, in complete turmoil. The person who stood now, just under six feet, was in possession of a type of mind which could pass from one to the other with a single idea, thought or contrivance as easily as turning off a light. He could changed his entire attitude and way of thinking. There were many ways this seemed a blessing, but some actions outweigh others.

At this moment he thought of nothing but what he would do tomorrow. These times he spent at Lake Tahoe were among the best of his young life. You could smell the very idea of the good life here along with the tinkling of wine glasses aside expensive shores.

Suddenly there came a switch in perception and he thought of it.

Was it happening again? Was he losing...?

He had tried to think of what a beautiful...

"Oh god," he said to himself, "not beautiful," with that he relinquished his current train of thought which sped directly back.

To her.

As had happened so often in the past forty eight hours, he had tried too hard. Now her face, her voice, her laugh, dominated him body and soul. He shook his head and looked around but nothing had changed.

The moon, directly above now, had long since shed its light to dance upon rippling water that caressed the beach.

Waves still came in, as if icing on a cake, spread out over and over, till the surface looked perfectly smooth.

Paul pulled his coat tighter to his waist and sat down again. All those stupid, crazy, triumphant, useless events rushed in on him from all sides.

Sighing heavily, he watched his breath vanish into the cool night air.

The fight to remain sane a few more hours was over. The loser sat on a rustic pier, on a lake in Northern California, trying to forget. The winner, though in the same place and time, had no choice but to recall.

Yes, it all came painfully back.

To both of them? He wondered.

She had once seemed the very breath of life to him. The one who would just as soon walk through sprinklers with him than go around them, and yet still stay sane enough to put up with all the high school bullshit.

Paul took the boat to shore.

He dropped the coin in the slot and dialed. He could imagine the scene in his mind as the phone rang once, twice: She would answer and all the feelings would come back to her, he'd hang up and pick up his bags. Driving would be too slow, so he'd feel the plane lift off the ground and rise toward new promises, new beginnings. He was smiling. Everything will work out.

Two hundred miles to the west a phone rang.

Jeff Richards answered the phone, "Hello?"

Paul hung up the phone.

PART 8 - SHE AWOKE

She awoke to the sound of the phone ringing. Jeff must have answered it. In the small bedroom she heard familiar rustling sounds. The morning sun filtered in through the drawn white shades as she got out of bed and walked over to the crib.

The baby had been up ten minutes and wanted its mother. She tried not to think about Paul as she tenderly picked up her son and held him close.

"It's okay", she said, "everything will be all right."

Yet, she knew it wouldn't be, because the feeling she now had in the pit of her stomach would not go away for a while. She was feeling sorry, stupid and small, all at once.

For the next few nights he would haunt her dreams.

◆ ◆ ◆

THE SIREN

He stood on the corner, ashen faced and lean looking. Knowing he blurred into and among the rest of these nameless hulks around him. He'd come to the city weeks ago. Out of time and out of money. He stood on what had to be the most congested corner. The young man leaned against a bench in what seemed to be the middle of the city. The noise of the city had reached a grimy crescendo in his mind as he stood, lost.

His mind raced with thoughts. What is my master? What would I sacrifice. Everything? To be able to really do it. In order for my creativity, my life, to be in full flux? I must get in touch with me, my health stems from this, my body is fragile and vulnerable. Take care and make it strong, make it well and more responsive, better shape, stamina. I will be twenty six. I will write every day. What stops me?

Sleep.

David realized how tire he was.

He was miserably tired.

He had been waiting for a long, long time.

He didn't have to wait any longer. The light had changed. Masses of people crossed the busy city street. It seemed he'd walked this block earlier this morning, only his despair was deeper now, his brow darker.

The comforting slant of soft summer afternoon light fell on him through the city skyline.

At the street light and crosswalk up ahead she walked into view. She smiled. A secret smile. He hadn't seen one in quite a while.

So he followed.

He was out of work, out of time, and now this inspiration! Small, slim and dark she moved through the crowd with intent and a purposeful walk. He followed her into an office building and the elevator where people were getting on and off. The people continued to leave at various floors until at last he is alone with her.

She was beautiful to him.

He didn't know if he should be frightened... then a flash. Feeling somewhere between the pleasure of Heaven the sins of Hell.

They were on the top floor now, two flights of stairs to the roof.

On the roof she stood near the edge. A short wall surrounded the roof in colorless stone, waist high and only a few feet thick. The sun was still up, though the wind chilled him.

"What are we doing here? Let's go down, I'll buy you a drink." Ouch! He'd heard that line fall crashing to the ground even as he spoke it. He wished he hadn't spoken at all. Besides, where was I going to get the money? She probably thinks I'm an idiot, he thought.

She didn't seem to notice. She was too busy looking at the city skyline.

He could not see her eyes clearly but her body seemed to tell him that she'd come to a decision. It was the way she straightened a little. Then she turned rapidly around. She walked toward him smiling again.

"There is no hope," her eyes looking right at his. She spoke even as her arm reached out to him and snaked around his neck.

"What?" he didn't know what was happening and didn't know this girl, but he noticed he wasn't moving or trying to get away.

"There is no hope and no reason for going on."

Suddenly he knew he should be far away from here. From her eyes, something about her presumed. She was like a dull narcotic slowly drowning his senses.

She was pressing against him now and her face was right there in front of him, a breath away from his.

"Why are you doing this?" he whispered.

"Why did you follow me?" was her reply.

She kissed him long and hard but somehow gentle too. He was annoyed at his own reaction. Subtle nuances he'd thought long vanished. He put her arms about the slimness of her waist and drew her even closer to him.

She broke away and backed quickly from him. She went to the short wall surrounding the roof.

"What are you doing?" he almost pleaded.

She lifted herself up and was sitting on the wall. His feet were firmly positioned.

He could not move.

"It's useless," she said as she righted herself, standing now. The wind was lifting her brown hair all about her face. She smoothed it back and out of the way with one hand and beckoned him to come over with the other hand.

He wanted her. It was getting more and more difficult to think of anything else. The tiniest shred of rationalization tried to make its way through his muddled thoughts. 'If I stand up there with her I can bring her down,' he thought. It was almost as if he had taken but a few short steps and he was there with her.

For some bizarre reason he felt safe. Like a last plea for sanity and real life. He felt alive in this precarious void. "It'll be dark soon. let's go down," he offered.

"Oh, we will," she paused to smile, "we'll leave all this behind," and saying this, she moved back a step, still holding hands. His entire body was slick with sweat. She was right on the edge.

"This is it," she let go of him. She stepped off the ledge and never stopped looking at him. She was still smiling even as she fell. The wind wrapped her hair and dress about her body.

The hair on his neck bristled. She kept staring at him, smiling as she fell in the stillness of approaching dusk, like a melancholy wave from a departing sea. He watched her fall off, down, down in stillness.

Transfixed by her smile and her red dress waving, he too stepped off.

He had been waiting for a long, long time. To feel. To fly away. All around him and high above him were the walls of this cavernous city. And for a time he flew past harsh lines of solid gray offices. Like citadels, palaces on high where people eked out existences in tiny offices... for a time.

Wind tugged at him while he continued to think of her smile. Trying to forget the silhouette of billowing waves of hair along her goodly lines.

He faced the larger void. He choked back the tears, grasping what would meet this reality. High above him another sky opened to him, while far below cars howled into canyons of steel and glass.

Down below, he heard himself.

As if a loud knock on a large door.

◆ ◆ ◆

ENTANGLED IN HER

Victoria looked at her watch again. Scott asked, "Are you sure we'll make it to the plane on time?"

"Sure," she said, flashing a smile. Probably a little more weakly than she'd wanted him to see. Through the streets of her city by the sea, they raced.

He was so quiet today. He tended to be when he was down.

There were so many things he wanted to say, but the silence hung over the conversation. Let's not think about that right now, he told himself.

"This is silly. Didn't I say that I would respect you and keep my distance?" he offered.

"Of course, but can't I still hear from you?" she asked.

"Sure," he said. He felt his resolve slipping, maybe for good. She was gaining ground.

She said, "Everything will be okay, it will work out."

But something hung in the background for him or for her or for both of them. Christ, what movie was this from? He thought to himself.

They passed an older woman drenched in finery and heavy perfume, her face twisted and fluffed; pampered into a mask of haughtiness, staring blankly out toward the plane. There was the start and stop of people waiting to board.

"How much do I have?" he asked.

"Excuse me?" the ticket agent replied.

"How much time until... before they start boarding?" he asked.

The airline ticket agent was short, stocky and annoyed. He glanced up from his 'busy' work and half scowled a reply, "They're boarding now, sir. You have about ten minutes."

"Thanks," Scott replied politely.

The sentence had been handed down.

Scott felt the tiny squeeze from the hand he held so gingerly in his own.

"We've still got some time," offered Victoria.

As the two of them moved towards an empty row of uncomfortable looking seats, she determinately took him by the hand, leading the way. As it's always been, he thought quietly. He noted that even though bright sunlight slashed through the huge window before them, creeping across the carpet in front of them, there was a definite chill to the air. He knew there would be today.

Outside, the sound of the airport droned on. They became silent for a moment letting time slip past, letting out a breath, composing goodbyes for each other. A tightness grew inside his chest. It was true then; you did catch your breath at times like these...

Victoria thought it was just about time for another cigarette. She nervously lit one and drew in a breath, carefully blowing the smoke out the side of her mouth. Nothing overwhelming or harsh, just the slightest hint of tobacco. He didn't like the fact that she smoked, not liking the idea at anything impairing her fragility. He also thought it made her look kind of sexy.

Her complexion was dark tan, as if some Renaissance painter had brushed the color onto her cheeks. The face Raphael and all the old masters had tried to capture; angelic and true. Fitzgerald could have written of her. He would have done justice to all the qualities that made up Victoria. Her hair was cut short, exposing that wonderful neck. Brunette curls, a childlike face, no harsh lines that had always seemed to him wise behind those eyes. Beyond the experiences of just one lifetime.

"We are in the middle of that 'month or two' away from each other," she decided.

"I'll be back at spring break. Your students must be jealous," Scott replied.

"They're not yet, I think they like you," she soothed.

"Write the story about your mom's childhood, I like the trapped in the attic stuff...." he said.

She asked, "Will you send me more poetry?"

"As soon as I've written some more...." he said.

"I think we've made a good start," she decided again. He searched her face for some hint of sarcasm but found none; only clear eyes and a strong resilience.

"Oh, I think so," he smiled too.

"I'll be thinking of you. I've had a good time," she commented.

"With the exercise we've been having, you look good," he replied with a smile.

"You're being strong for me, aren't you?" she asked.

"No. For me," he said finally. He kissed her now. Like their first kiss, tentative and holding back a bit.

She took his arm and began walking to the gate.

"Well, there. They've said their goodbyes. Does she go home and think of him?" she asked with a dramatic flourish.

"Yes, she should try and continue her life, routine, normally..." he joined in.

"Exactly. She's still not sure why he has to go, he could work anywhere in California," she offered.

"Hmm, he could stay with her...?" his hope rose.

"Now you're being sentimental," she said.

"Hey, I'll take sentimental anytime," he replied.

"We should rewrite that goodbye at the house, the way my voice got shaky," she reminded him.

"Yes," was all he could think to say.

He stopped to look hard into her eyes. To remember. He set the suitcase down and held her in his arms, about her waist. She were still looking forward, toward the exit signs. She tried to think of something to delay him before she had to go down the escalator, on a different path.

He told her quietly, "I guess I'd better... really... get on board now."

She kissed him much more intently and sure, "springtime, then?"

"Springtime," He took her hand and placed it on his chest, "you're right here," he said and looked at her.

She smiled and cocked her head playfully, "I like that line," she said.

"Okay?" he asked.

"Okay," she surrendered, "goodbye."

"I... I do have to go," he said.

"I love you," she said finally.

"I love you too," he said as he pulled her to him and kissed her. One long eternal minute, suspended.

It was over too quickly. His head pounded almost wishing he could leave now without saying goodbye. Forget the one last time, to kiss her again before parting. The sunlight filtered in low as the sound of the plane's engines droned on, wailing as they picked up speed.

The ticket agent said, "Sir, you're going to have to hurry."

He looked in her eyes once again, one last time. She hugged him quickly with a faint smile of remembering and sadness.

"Take care," she offered.

With a blur of motion, walking away from her graceful intensity, staring fixedly on the doorway before him he walked away.

He didn't look back.

~~~

It seemed so long ago now, as if a thousand miles lay between now and the last time she had smiled at him. Somewhere over northern California between the stale crackers and his second drink he read the note. It had been placed carefully in his screenwriting book. Penned by a steady hand while he'd been catching a few more minutes sleep that morning. Not in her grocery list scrawl, but a steady determined hand.

She was 'the one', to borrow a coin from the phrase. Did she know that? Probably depended on the company she kept. At any given moment flirtatious, yes, but not obviously so. He liked that. Yet there was definitely a sparkle; a knowing when a man approached her as if she were saying to herself something like, "Ah, there you are. I've expected you." How many men had told her how beautiful she was? It was scary...too many numbers for a guy like me, he thought.

Why do I feel overwhelmed in her presence? She's a class act, way out of my league. Like when she asked me, "Do you like your name Scott?" when the conversation began to drag a little. With too many empty spaces and long pauses, she pops up with that one. A voice low and full of deep resonances; not just in the timbre itself but in the very meaning behind the question.

He remembered that morning when she had stood in the open doorway and stared at the sea. It always seemed to soothe her... the waves rolling, heaving in upon themselves in majestic green contemplation.

Her eyes were that same color and just as majestic. Alarmingly quiet eyes, not quick to dart from here to there in nervous glances, but long, lingering and secure when they looked upon you.

The face that had turned back towards him was young and fair. It was almost haunting the way she smiled at him now. And suddenly, he thought, I recognized that gaze from dreams I'd had of her. Graced by a mild attentiveness that grew stronger by the day.

Now the room grew louder with the silence we had been avoiding until now. Before the drive to the airport.

~~~

At his layover, he sat in a soft shaft of afternoon light that illuminated one corner of the lounge, nursing the latest in a series of rum & Cokes. He was not in the habit of drinking this early in the day but these circumstances were quite beyond his control. He precluded that a stiff belt would make a stiffening of the 'old resolve'.

As he let another swallow of the drink burn its way down the back of his throat, the terminal loudspeakers seemed to grow diminished in volume. Announcing in its monotonous drone the various incoming (hellos) and departing daily (dearly) departed.

He closed his eyes and saw again what had been there for days now. Her face had not gone the way of everyday memories and wanderings of the mind. She smiled at him in the same sharpness and clarity which he'd seen the last time in another airline terminal, far to the north but not so far that he couldn't summon them now.

The waitress appeared, "Had enough?"

"I don't..." he paused as if to double check himself, "...think so", he said turning up the empty glass.

~~~

He was coming home. Then again not home, but to a remembrance. He never really lived here, just became part of something that remains here still. 'Here', just another name for a small town on the Pacific Coastline. Nestled in the fertile valley, it's grown too much but it hasn't shrunk. His car eases hesitantly towards the center of this town where he grew up chasing girls in fast circles.

From every part of town his place can be seen, standing majestic, not quite reaching for the clouds.

Are you giving up? he thought. Yes, just for a while. But soon enough, I'll have another plane to catch in Frisco.

The tall rusted iron gate laid tossed aside allowing enough room to pass. I would think they'd made a museum or something, but people forget...

Later, he'd been going through old boxes and happened upon some photographs of her. At first he treated it as just another odd find, not really paying the discovery much attention. Little by little however, he found himself returning to those faded pictures. Memories he'd thought just as faded, were suddenly sharpened and secure again.

He tried to write again.

This time the pages of blank paper that lay before him did not seem so formidable. The alcohol had been sufficiently purged from his body and he felt his mind clearing for the first time in days. He picked through the rumpled sheets of prose and poetry stacked not so neatly on the table.

Then she smiled in his mind from far, far away. It seemed to him another part of him melted, then drifted towards her, wanting her in all possible degrees in that one pure and intense moment.

He wrote from memory (or memories, if you will) remembering, if not the exact words, at least the order in which they should be placed...

~~~

Before it had been a simple matter of closing his eyes and conjuring up her face, imagining a fragrance or listening for her laughter in the back of his mind.

Now, however, she was here. Very palpable, warm and constant.

He thought of the two of them lying in the next room listening for a moment, as if like a parent, both checking for the steady breathing of a sleeping child.

She was so right for him.

She was all that a woman could be to him. She represented the most wonderful mixture of quiet beauty and fragile self-assuredness. It was all he could do to keep from holding her close to him just to feel the pulse of her vitality. She would forever walk in a certain angelic light, as far as he was concerned.

When he found himself staring at her, taking in all of what she was about, he always readied himself to avert his eyes. He knew to look into her eyes was an overwhelming mixture of loss, hope, intensity and love.

Ah, but to be lost in those eyes.

He turned to see her standing with her back to him and was about to ask her what was wrong when the low hum of the stereo interrupted his question. What had indeed only been a barely audible whisper was now quite decipherable. The steady bass beat of "Every Breath You Take" drifted through his house as it had so often in the last two months.

Only now, she was here.

She straightened a bit and continued to stare out towards the window as if the answers lay outside in the descending darkness amongst the trees. She sensed this was the song he listened to when he thought of her. To think of all the poems and letters that may have been written to his siren, like the lyrics shook her resolve.

Seemingly, there was no air left in the small living room as he maneuvered around the sofa, carefully choosing his steps, until he stood directly behind her.

He breathed the fragrance of her in, sweet jasmine; light and so delicate he could die now and not put up much of a fight, he thought romantically. Wait... not die... not just yet... later, later. There would be time enough for that. Right now...

He put his hands on her shoulders. They seemed so tiny now, fragile. She leaned back against him ever so slightly.

"Do you want me to stop?" he asked.

"Stop... Loving me?" she asked back.

Now he turned her around towards him, at last. Her face was close to his and he could almost feel the warmth of her blush.

"No. Stop... desiring you. I want to love you, but I am definitely losing some of the nobleness I had about how I want to start," he responded.

His arms slipped around her waist, her arms about his shoulders.

"Never..." she began, moving her quite exquisite mouth closer to his, "...ever... stop."

They kissed, and as it deepened, the smallest most tender cry sprang from inside her. It was a sound he'd been waiting to hear for a long time.

He answered her with more kisses.

◆ ◆ ◆

THE ENEMY ADVANCES

The main dining room of the plush restaurant resembles a quiet field before a great battle. Silent tables and chairs wait to be abused and handled as weapons of war. The newly vacuumed carpet, laid out, readies itself to be trampled on. Now music is piped in through hidden speakers to create the perfect atmosphere. The stage is set now, as the head waiter deploys his men to strategic positions.

Automatically, the doors open to admit the shoving, moaning enemy. Customers file in and grab for seats, while busboys receive orders to move forward. Finally satisfied with their location, patrons begin to order dinner in defiant tones.

"...and make my steak medium rare, not burnt to a crisp like the last time!"

"Yes sir," is all the waiter can reply to the stuffy old man. The clatter of glasses and dishes spring from the hot kitchen. Time goes by and the air fills with smells of steak, chicken and roast beef. Apparently, this tames hostile tempers. What should have been a fierce confrontation becomes a muffled, satisfied roar.

Dinner is finished, and waitresses clear away plates and wounded comrades. The carpet once bright red is strewn with napkins and bits of food. By the time the attacking army has left and paid the dues, all is calm. The night is hardly over though, for each side begins to prepare for another frontal assault.

And only one side has fresh soldiers.

◆ ◆ ◆

TOUGH TO BE A MAN

He sat alone in the cool of the kitchen, humming some old Cole Porter song about falling in love.

The bottle of whiskey was half empty and he held it with a quaking hand. The face I saw before me, held all the pain and anguish I thought it could possess or endure. His formally clean-shaven taut face had given way to a black rough beard. Occasionally he rubbed his reddened nose. It looked broken.

Night had long since dropped her black curtain to enshroud the farm. I could still hear the frogs and crickets chirping in their melancholy way, just beyond the battered screen door.

Standing in the quiet darkness I watched him nod off. My mother and sisters were asleep upstairs not aware of the late hour or our visitor. I was glad I was the only one here. Now, alone with him, we wouldn't have to pretend. Maybe we could really talk.

It seemed all my fifteen years had borne their burden on me that night; taken their toll on the happy carefree days of childhood. Responsibility was all mine now, since he had left.

As I walked toward him, though, all at once I felt like a little boy again.

Into the kitchen with its high ceiling and flaking paint I moved, slowly, deliberately onward. The dishes were stacked high and all the drain boards and counters were covered by a fine grime.

I could feel my bare feet stick to the floor with each step as I inched closer, pulling the robe around me nervously.

He looked up and acted as if he were seeing me from far away. Those large brown eyes had once sparkled like the promise of a dawning sun.

Now they glistened beneath thick pools of tears. Yet, from that haggard face there broke a familiar, wide smile.

"Pa?" I half whispered, "where have you been?"

His smile faded into a expression that seemed one part remorse and one part satisfaction...

"Places you shouldn't know about."

"Ma's been worried sick," I said in an almost whiny voice.

A glint of recognition, as he pulled me over to the chair beside him.

"Your Ma. How is she?" he asked pausing to cough the sick cough of an alcoholic.

"She moped around a spell, but she's tried to forgot. Plus there's the baby across the way to take care of now."

"Oh," he sighed, and took a long drink from the bottle. Sweet and delicious he made it seem.

"Where did they take you?" I inquired, not innocently.

His feet shuffled, and then I heard them. I poked my head beneath the oak table and saw the chains. They were suspended between his ankles.

"The gang?" I asked, almost proudly.

"Yes."

"Why Pa?"

"They say I killed a man," he growled.

"Did you?"

The father I remembered might have hit me. The father here now just stood up.

"I don't know why I came back here," he began, "because the boss man is after me. But I am cunning, boy."

"Why did you come back?" I asked.

"Hmmm... Maybe it's that I wanted to sit here and soak in all those sweet memories I know I can never have again. Maybe it's that I wanted to see you and tell you not to be like me. Go to school, boy and learn as much as you can. Never find yourself in these."

He pointed to the chains.

Pa picked up the coat and pulled it tight around himself.

"Its gonna be light in a few minutes," he figured as he put a big roughened hand on my shoulder. Then moving toward the door...

"Let's go to the barn. You can help me outta these son, and I'll be much obliged if you grab some food for me."

Moments later the sun was peeking between the willows and the cool mist of morning rolled across the yard.

"Thanks boy," he said, throwing the axe to the side. Rubbing his swollen feet he laughed that big ornery laugh I'd heard in summertime, swimming at the pond. He looked at me in a way he never had before.

"You know, I'd never think to see you up this early before."

I smiled and handed him the paper bag with bread and fruit in it.

"Well nowadays I have to," I said imitating him the best I could.

Then we both laughed.

Father and son, we stood holding each other and rocked back and forth.

He straightened up and shook my hand as he towered over me in the morning sun.

"Remember what I told you, and... don't tell your Ma I was here. I've put her through enough."

"I won't, sir."

"Call me Sam."

"I won't... Sam", I shivered, ready to bust out crying.

But I didn't.

"Take care Jackson," he said.

He began north, toward the thick woods.

I stood on the porch watching him whoop and holler, free as a bird. The last time I saw him he was singing again.

Then he was gone.

A while later, Ma came out the screen door with a fresh load of clothes.

"Boy? what are you doing out so early with just your robe on?"

"Just watching, Ma."

"Watching for what?" she asked impatiently.

"Nothing Ma, nothing I guess."

And that was that.

I never saw my father again but I remember honoring his memory.

When Buck Jones said he'd heard they caught my Pa and strung him up, I hit him and damn near busted his head wide open. That was in a bar in Atlanta, on my twenty first birthday.

Even then it was tough to be a man.

◆ ◆ ◆

FORESHADOWING OF THE END

He had taken a few days off from school to go climbing and hiking up into the woods above Seattle. A proper study for my English literature thesis, he thought. The first two nights passed eventually, but on Friday night a full moon rose over scraggy pine tops. A wind bellowed down the natural funnels of the mountains.

That's the last thing he remembered before the darkness took him.

"What's her problem?" the nurse said.

The other nurse looked up from her paperwork.

"Her boyfriend is in that room. He was in a camping accident about six weeks ago. Fell off an embankment or something. Crushed vertebra. He's been comatose. They didn't know if he'd pull through.

"She's been here every day. Sometimes twice a day. Didn't see her yesterday, though."

"He came out of the coma yesterday?" asked the other nurse.

"Yeah. But, from what I understand, sometimes there's a memory loss..."

"So, she's the girlfriend? His mother told me they only met six months ago."

"Damn visitors anyway."

Lynn, think about it, she told herself. She'd been coming here for the last month and a half.

"It's alright," she said under her breath.

"You can go right in, miss," the nurse offered.

"Thank you," was all Lynn said, opened the door and went in. She absent-mindedly smoothed out another imaginary wrinkle and adjusted her hem for the hundredth time.

"Who are you?" he groaned.

Lynn turned sharply, eyes flashing, darting to his face. He had opened his eyes to see her standing in the artificial light and the cool shadows they made, wearing a knit sweater and skirt that clung to her slender form.

"It's me, Lynn."

He didn't say anything for a long time, studying her face.

"Excuse me miss, but I don't know you... or at least... I don't remember you."

Lynn turned, eyes flowing, "it's alright."

He paused again, "and it's nice to meet you. Sorry if..."

"No, It's not you... my name is Lynn... goodbye."

She could get used to anything, save that familiar hospital staleness to the air. The cold smell that hospital rooms get for the recovering or terminally ill. Paler, so pale his blond hair looked today. A face tanned and laughing not two days before the accident. Why hadn't she said yes when he asked her to go camping?

She was trying to figure out who in the hell she was. What *she* wanted.

Now he was awake and didn't remember her.

She had to remember that he was not the man whom she had been mad at before the accident. She was mad that she didn't know who to be upset with. Right on cue his mother walked into the hallway.

"Hello, Cherie."

"Oh, hello there... Lynn."

"Did you know he's awake?" Lynn asked

"Of course." Cherie said.

"Everyone else knew about this before I did?" asked Lynn.

"Well, we felt..." Cherie began.

Lynn wondered who the 'we' was. Be polite... be polite, "I was the last to know. Why? Why didn't the nurses tell me?" the young woman stopped and looked back towards the nursing station with an almost murderous glance.

"You're not immediate family, dear. They were only doing their job," Cherie said.

"Damn those nurses anyway, all they thought about was their job," said Lynn.

"I've been here all day. Have you seen him today?" Cherie asked.

"Yes, That's how I knew. But I'm the man's girlfriend, alright?" Lynn looked for the slightest glimmer of hate in his mother's eyes... and couldn't find it, "listen, Cherie, I'm sorry. I know how tough this has been for everyone. I was just a little shocked, you know?"

"I know Lynn. If it helps I did leave a message for you to call me."

Lynn remembered now. The phone message recorder, "Hi Lynn, this is Cherie..." Lynn had stopped the machine. I will call later, she thought. Something had been nagging at her at the time, but she couldn't pin it down. She had told herself 'I'm so busy,' I need to find a babysitter for tomorrow, I need to make a hairstylist appointment... it would wait until morning...the rest of the messages, she just didn't want to hear anymore. Who knows what the rest of them would have done to her.

"Well, I'm going in now..." said Cherie.

"Of... of course. I'll go home now. I will come back in the morning," Lynn said.

"Goodnight," Cherie said as she walked to his room.

"Goodnight," Lynn said.

On Lynn's way home, a million thoughts swirled. She remembered the early morning on her first visit. Fluffing up pillows, arranging the flowers in the room. Trying not to cry over his broken body. We were so happy. The small plaintive cry, cut off for some reason, a voice so far away.

The morning light slanted in between venetian blinds and threw rippled shadows along the length of the bed.

"Hello, there," she said.

He blinked once, and then smiled at her, "Hi."

"This is a little strange," she said.

"Very," he agreed.

She moved closer to the bed as he shifted position.

"Do you know how long you've been awake?" asked Lynn.

"Since yesterday. The doctors came in to examine me, ask me questions... I will have a long road back, but I should walk in time... and then Mom came bursting in crying and all that," his voice trailed off.

"Yeah," she said and pulled a chair, sat beside him. At last a break, a common subject.

"I just found out yesterday. I was mad... well, pissed off, really, that they waited so long to tell me."

"I was thinking about how weird it must have been for you... um... Lynn? There are times when I'll see you in my mind, and think I remember things," he only wished he knew who she was.

"How about you? Having some stranger come in every day," she said.

He was getting good at this, he thought. Not quite remembering every detail, but a few images returned. An insatiable desire to know her so that he could recall her later. They talked for a few more minutes, her trying subtle references to things he might remember.

"I just moved out of my apartment, finally," she offered.

"Oh, good for you," he offered in return, "I think... I could fall in love with you right now, today and all over again."

"I feel like... like I am talking to a good friend, not a boyfriend," she seems confused, "but I... I am empty."

"What?" he was confused, but something began to click in his mind.

"Don't... can you understand?"

"No," he said firmly.

He took her by the hand and held it tightly as if the intensity of his emotions would be channeled through their touch, "Passion. Do you know what that is?" he asked her.

"What are you...?" she began.

"I love you, Lynn," he said to her in a quiet voice, then in afterthought he told her, "I've worked my way up. now I only have to tell you that every six weeks."

She smiled. Her saddest expression, one he had gotten used to seeing just before the accident.

"I need some..." she stopped abruptly, "this is going to sound melodramatic and silly."

"No it wouldn't. Just the same, don't say it."

She tried to smile at him.

"I wish I could say 'shall we begin again'?"

"Yes, do, by all means."

"I need... and you too... I need to be by myself and away from everybody. You need time to yourself to heal."

She stopped when he let go of her hand. She shrunk away from his grasp. He had been angry with her for not feeling the same way he felt that night, six weeks before. So he went camping alone. He suddenly remembered it all. Now he felt the familiar hollow feeling in the pit of his stomach.

"I have been somebody's 'something' all my life; daughter, student, girlfriend. I don't know how to be somebody's nurse."

With bleary eyed complacency he lied and agreed it wasn't worth the trouble, "understanding the circumstances, I guess that would be the best for both of us."

"Besides, before I'd felt like I had just started a new adventure, now it's been like talking with a old friend," she said awkwardly.

"Yeah, me to," there would be no fighting back time then, he thought. She must have been thinking of this before I left that night, he realized.

"The key is that I will be a strong, determined woman at the end of this. I don't know what it is I want... but I deserve the right to take the time to figure it out."

"If it's because I didn't remember you right away."

"No, not that simple or cruel... oh, what time is it?" she asked suddenly.

Back to reality, he thought, "It's 2:30."

"I'll be late. I better get going," she said.

"Yeah... I guess I am a little tired," he lied.

She bent over and kissed him lightly on the cheek, "Take care," she whispered.

"Bye," he replied. She was already gone.

She had left the room. There was no fighting back her tears. She knew what she had said was not quite all true. She had the buffer of dimmed recollections to call up, vividly. Still, it would not be easy to start over.

It was not until her footsteps began to fade down the darkening corridor that the two young nurses resumed their intense discussions of what makes a good relationship and what they expected from theirs.

He sat in the cool room collecting his thoughts. He would always remember thinking that he should have written everything down. Each episode a story on its own. Fragments, now he could only touch on certain feelings. It was not necessarily what was actually said but more of what he felt.

He found himself closing his eyes and fighting off images, faces. If only I could have this.... if only I had done it this way. It was almost a peaceful feeling, a pleasant pressure that held him now, knowing at least he could survive this.

◆ ◆ ◆

THE POOL
AND JONATHAN SMYTHE

It looked like a road few had traveled on, thought Jonathan Smythe.

The heat rose from the valley floor and seemed to engulf his every step. As far as the young man could see the desert stretched to infinity on either side of the highway. From his disbelieving eyes, it rose out towards the horizon like some woman's sublime figure had traveled across the Desert Valley floor itself.

It was a blistering heat. Sweat broke through every pore of his body. Engulfed, every step was labored. The scorching sun upon him, he wiped his forehead with a brush of his already soaked sleeve...

Then it just appeared.

As he trudged past the ancient broken gate, he paused to lean against a pillar that once must have held the gate. Hell could not have been hotter, he thought as he paused to blink the sweat from the corners of eyes. He walked past the entrance and down the road.

He spotted the old man, "Hey old-timer!" was all he could think to say. Dust seemed to have settled permanently on the old man's faded work clothes. He greeted Jonathan with a grimy smile.

"Its hotter than hell, isn't it?" Jonathan smiled weakly.

"Well..." began the old man, who then stopped, and began to smile too. As if something had suddenly struck him funny.

A laugh that Smythe could have sworn was no more than an old hag's cackle.

"My car," gulp, "it broke down just off the highway. Got to be in Phoenix by tonight."

Then he saw the pitcher of water in an open air shack a few feet behind the old man. The pitcher was full of iced water that formed beads of sweat that rolled down the walls of the glass pitcher.

The old man followed his gaze. He smiled a feral smile through yellowed teeth and piercing gray eyes. A face that for an instant looked monstrously evil, then settled into the tranquility of an old man's features. He looked so cool, Jonathan through, as if he had stepped from a long, cold shower. Smythe closed his eyes and banished the thought as impossible, "I followed the road until I felt I would drop from sheer exhaustion..."

The old man turned his back and walked toward the shack. Smythe followed him towards the shack and the pitcher of water. Great stacks of yellow newspapers and dusty photos covered the musty, withered walls inside. He spotted a fan on a table. He reached to turn it on.

"That damn fan won't work!" said the old man. Just then a hot gust of wind tore through the shack, "Oww...

ouch!" His hand jerked back as red spots appeared before his eyes.

Then Jonathan followed the old man's gaze, past the pitcher and the fan, out toward the back. He looked out the back of the grimy shack.

The pool glistened crystal blue in the noon time blaze of day.

"Your soul?" Smythe thought he heard the old man say.

"What was that?" asked Smythe.

"You swim?" the old man asked.

That grin again.

For no reason, panic slowly rose in him.

"Nice, ain't it?" continued the old man, as they both stared at the pool.

It was mesmerizing.

The old man was still talking, "Got some swim trunks for sale, just got to sign for them."

"Hmmm?" Smythe replied weakly as he stared at the cool blue pool.

"Can I get those trunks for you?"

"Sure, great," Smythe said.

"Here you go, just sign the parchment below... here... that's good," the old man trailed off.

Smythe had never felt water like this. As he entered the water he imagined a Caribbean sea. Perfectly clean, pure. As he dunked his head under, he saw the old man staring at him from the pools edge. That smile again.

He went under the blue, then he come up gasping for air. He felt something wrap around his ankle and pull him down. He struggled up and thrashed about but by then all about him had changed, decayed.

All about him was red.

◆ ◆ ◆

THE LAST GUNFIGHTER

It was a Friday night in March. As usual depression was about fall on Ryne like the proverbial ton of bricks. The idea of the single life hardly intrigued him, but lately he had been contemplating a career in a monastery. Just kidding, he thought... at least he hoped that was a joke. He *could* go see his sister, brother-in-law and niece in Phoenix this weekend. He could drive back Sunday night. That would avoid the "weekend scene" altogether.

It did his mind good to drive the one hundred and twenty miles through the desert, clearing the cobwebs, so to speak. Take chances! Live and be a part of the world! Be done with internalizing so much. Take delight in the world about you. Learn to live... take a stab... a shot at life! It might slap back from time to time but it won't eat you alive. Being more adventurous won't hurt you!

As he drove, he was reminded of a funny story his friend Phil had told him. Phil said there was this old guy who hangs out at this one gas station in the desert. He dresses in full western gear. He has an intense eye contact and a surly mood. Phil told him this guy will suddenly take out his forefinger and thumb like it was a gun.

Phil described this sad old man as 'very short with steel grey eyes, and a glint of sadness.' Ryne could not forget that line. "Calls himself Mr. Luke Short, I kid you not. Don't draw on him, though," Phil said with mock seriousness.

"Don't worry, I won't, I'll play it safe," Ryne had returned in the same tone.

As the blue of dusk approached, he neared that very gas station. Perfect, he thought, I need gas anyway.

He pulled up to the curb by the gas pump, just to the left of a rusting flagpole. He got out of the car to the smell of orange blossoms. Sure enough, he saw the tiny man. He had a strange feeling he had meet him before. Opening the passenger door he noticed his stereo had been turned up nearly all the way. From the radio, the DJ said in whispered reverence, "An Innocent Man" by Mr. William Joel...'

"Alright, innocent man!" he said out loud.

He sang along. He almost turned it up louder but then thought better of it, wouldn't want to blow the poor old-timer's eardrums.

He put the gas nozzle in and went to the old man, "I am here for Phil," he said. A short wheeze issued from inside the old man's throat as he gave a tip of his hat to Ryne as a gesture.

Ryne could not resist having a little fun. He hoped he would not scare the old man too much, "Mr. Short, what do you think?" Ryne stiffened up his index finger and thumb and immediately slipped out his imaginary six shooter. Ryne smiled.

Before Ryne could apologize for his silly brashness he heard a loud 'click-bang.' Suddenly his chest hurt. The smell of orange blossoms was gone now, replaced by the faint odor of gun powder. His chest burned as if he'd inhaled a room full of smoke.

As the second bullet ripped into his chest he found himself amazed at how fast the old guy's movements had been. Having produced a Colt pistol from underneath the dusty black coat, Ryne may have been beaten on the draw, but he still might survive the gunfight. Steel grey eyes - yes, but sad? My ass, Ryne thought.

Ryne had just enough time to stagger back and mutter "Jesus," before the third and final bullet punctured his left lung with the intent to kill. He was falling now and grabbing at his executioner's arm.

Mr. Short's shiny gun was still smoking. As it should be, Ryne reasoned. Ryne fell to the ground with a clattering noise. As the scene unfolded from his now topsy-turvy angle, he saw bespeckled blue dots.

People surrounded him them on all sides.

'Thanks for the warning, Phil,' he thought, laying crumpled against the stone curb. He could hear Phil in his head reply, 'you knew better, pal.'

He was surprised he was still alive. For an instant he wondered if he might even make it. But now he felt that magical band we tie around the living, slip loose.

'Dear dad... ' he thought, composing a letter in his mind, 'looks like I won't be able to make the trip back to

California after all. Signed, your currently dying son, Ryne.'

Something about that made him laugh. He thought of life. Sometimes it certainly does slap back. He was actually laughing up until the moment he died.

◆ ◆ ◆

LOST INFLUENCE

The following transcript is from a panel discussion on the cult following of the science fiction books and short stories of Ryne S. Torres. Mr. Torres was an early trailblazer of science fiction in the 1930's through the late 1950's. The moderator is Larry Bryan.

LARRY: Hello everyone, welcome to the first... well...yes, I'd say first... and certainly most prestigious panel on the Science Fiction stories of Ryne Scott Paul Torres. His work is well known and respected among classic Sci-fi nuts and scholars, but strangely less known to the general public. Let's get right to it. Our panel included:

World famous science fiction author **Scott McBrian-Faraday,** Stanford Professor of Sociology **Victoria Davenport,** poet laureate and author of over twenty bestselling books **Anson Jennings,** and to round us out is Mr. Torres' great niece and well known author in her own right, **Jennifer Tarkington.**

LARRY: Let's begin with you Ms. Tarkington. Why isn't your great uncle Ryne Scott Paul Torres more well known?

TARKINGTON: Well that is the mystery. He wrote alongside the greats of early science fiction like Asimov, Heinlein, Clarke. It's said that Clarke's inspiration for inventing the satellite came from Ryne when he showed him how bees fly in perfect orbits around trees. But there seems to be a wall around his access to fame...

JENNINGS: I think it had a lot to do with his background. He was born in 1916, in war-torn Europe during the Great War in Zaragoza, Spain. His influences were many and varied. He grew up all over. Spain, India, Australia, and of course England. There's a great story - legend really, that a young Ryne Torres snuck into the discussion group 'The Inklings', where J.J.R. Tolkien and C.S. Lewis were members. Legend says he and J.R.R. went out drinking that night and Ryne convinced Tolkien to use just his initials on *The Hobbit*. Ryne had published his first short story under Ryne S. P. Torres. The story goes that J.R.R. was going to publish under "John Ronald", his first and middle name. J.R.R. in turn convinced C.S. Lewis to use his initials as well. Amazing! He's always hanging around the club, but never a member.

LARRY: Fascinating. What a wide influence Torres had on what we take for granted today. Now a treat. A reading from Ryne Torres' Book *Commander North Rises:*

North looked at his second in command and the five others. Responsibility was something he had lived in the service of for the last ten years.

The Valiant was now the size of a pin-head, and final go-ahead was imperative. The memuturization technique developed three years ago was a long way from perfect.

Any size smaller than this, the captain was required to act on his own. He should weigh all possible considerations, for the technique could hardly guarantee success at this stage.

'It's almost like Russian roulette,' someone had once said.

North banished this from his mind and gave his orders to the impatient crew.

"Well people," he began, "the mission of the Valiant is to explore the edge of the next galaxy. We're going farther than last time... further than anybody so far, so I order," he concluded, "that this mission is a go."

This was followed by a energetic rumble.

The Deck officer confirmed, "alright then, the Valiant is go for final stage," Thirty seconds later Valiant could not have been seen with an X-1500 electron microscope. Let alone the naked eye.

Every time Commander Timothy North found himself shrinking to the size roughly equal to a single atom, he could not help but think he was alone in the universe.

After the initial shock to the system had passed, he opened his eyes and found he was not.

LARRY: Wow. Taking *Fantastic Voyage* style ideas to the next level. Asimov wrote the paperback novel based on the 1966 screenplay, which in turn had been borrowed from a Ryne Torres idea. Truly awesome.

DAVENPORT: Speaking of great stories and influences. Ayn Rand tells a story in her biography of meeting Torres not long after she came to America from Russia. Her Russian name was Alisa. She said that she got his autograph at a book signing. Well, Ryne was notorious for his varied handwriting - some of his original manuscripts are meticulous, some are nearly impossible to read. To Ayn, the autograph looked like it said "Ryn," which in his handwriting looked a lot like Ayn. And That's how she picked her new American name.

North Rises was one of my favorites. Although I would have to say that the sequel, *North of Nowhere* has one of my favorite passages:

...this thought floated in the back of his mind. The Valiant was the best ship in the fleet, its sleek graceful outline silhouetted against the universe.

It had the crew it deserved too, he thought. Each of the six members he owed his life to at one point or another.

Life. Life was something precious to a space monger, or to any man. A family to come home to, and a soft, quiet woman to soothe you.

"Commander," he said with more urgency.

"Hmmm, oh... sorry Roy, just thinking," he said.

"Yes sir, Mission Central has asked for the final go ahead."

LARRY: Mr. Faraday, what do you think Ryne's greatest contribution to the Sci-fi world was?

FARADAY: That's a tough one - there are so many: Domed cities, hovercraft, the far-sightedness of both Russia's rise and decline. But, for me, the floating time capsule cities always caught my imagination. Here's a short passage from the short story *The Floating Wake*:

"We have built this group of cities to float free in space until some intelligence finds them. The benefits that an alien intelligence will find our culture is fair compensation for our deaths."
"You mean there are more than one of these things skipper?"
"Yes, Dr. Andropov, it says here that apparently this pod was detached from the rest of the group. Who knows where they all are now!"

JENNINGS: As an author I'm always taken by his inventiveness - using small moments to build character or using the same character to define different ideas. Here's another scene from *North of Nowhere*:

Twelve hours earlier North had said goodbye to the three things which held him together. The two small boys had long since departed, giving their three legged pet more priority than daddy's trip.

Now, just his wife remained. He knew the old routine was about to begin.

"What can I say this time?" he pleaded.

"Just that you'll come back," she whispered. He touched her lips, the lips that were shining in the fading sunlight.

"I can't promise," he said, "you know that."

"Yes," she sighed.

A good woman he thought. I don't think she could stand anymore sentimentalities now, whatever she may say, not after that last mission.

Goodbye. So final. That damn word, he thought.

Whatever he might say, she wouldn't hear, and wouldn't want to.

LARRY: We've talked about his gift for looking forward. He also predicted consumerism, commercialization of space, even where the future U.S. space program would be headquartered...

It was cold on the way to Mission Control. Riding in the hover craft he looked below and wondered why it hadn't moved in centuries.

Houston had held the honor of being at the core of science in the United States. It was the birthplace of the primitive rockets that carried men to the now large colonies on the Moon and Mars.

What would it have been like being the first on an alien piece of rock? No, they weren't so alien now. Tourist traps or resorts have become more prominent. Much more than imaginary monsters.

He had no more time to think, for the hovercraft had set down. After unfastening his seat belt he moved toward the latch, while the stewardess gave her usual courtesy.

The administration building was always cold to him. Just like the day.

TARKINGTON: I've always appreciated his scope - his ability to set stories in the near future and the distant future. For instance: The Galactic Academy in *Academy Armada and the Alpha problem* was founded in 3012. While others cross paths with our timeline. For instance, he used the North character in the 21st century and his descendants in the 31st century. And he's not afraid to be controversial:

July 2019

"T minus 30 minutes and counting," the garbled voice boomed through the Houston Space Craft Center. Man's first voyage to Mars had come despite the cutbacks and protests. Proctor's face was full of triumph and pride as he helped with fuel consumption checks. This was his baby and America's

glory. Yes, those dammed Russians had fallen behind since the second revolution. Famine and tension had broken out. The emperor had abdicated and disappeared, the whole country was in turmoil.

Probably jealous and burning up with hate, he thought to himself. They had hung onto a bit of technology.... suddenly something foreign hit his stomach: fear. Could the Russians sabotage the mission for the sake of revenge? There were five men in that capsule, their lives were in his hands, would he be able to....no. No, he decided they were too far gone.

At that moment a meteor of measurable size entered earth's atmosphere and began to descend towards Greenland. Yet radar technicians all the world over didn't pay much attention. They were too busy watching America launch its first manned Mars landing, fifty years to the date of the first moon landing.

FARADAY: And remember, this was written in 1943. He even guesses the month and year of the moon landing! He also wasn't afraid to create massive destruction and write his way out of it. In 1943, he's predicting nuclear holocaust. Before Fat Man and Little Boy were even dropped.

"I can't help but suggest complete retaliation, Mr. President," Proctor said heavily.

He dropped the phone, "Nuclear war has commenced," said the intercom, "eight nuclear warheads have been launched deep into Russian soil... still no word from them."

One hour later, the teletype produced this: "We have been wrongly attacked by you. We had no knowledge of your craft's launch or destruction. Suggest you look at coordinated attack from elsewhere. But not before we taste revenge..."

The last line didn't come as a thunderbolt. It had been in the back of his mind all along.

TARKINGTON: Yes, but as bleak as he occasionally got, there was always hope. He believed firmly in the ideas of Humanity and Freedom.

...all major military installations have been destroyed in the United States, along with Hawaii. More later...

Proctor clicked the radio off, "the end of civilization and the world. Did not think I would see it, not even my kids..."

"Yeah," Reed said, "One country falls and the others follow suit."

A knock came at the door, it opened and the radar controller walked in. He looked as pale as death.

"What's the matter now?" Proctor demanded.

"Look," was all the controller said.

Procter took the sheet of paper. It was a missile trajectory layout he had seen many times before.

"You see," the controller started, "there and there," he pointed.

"The missile had come from Greenland, not Russia," he continued slowly, "we attacked out of sheer ignorance and stupidity..."

Proctor interrupted, "Now we'll pay for this terrible mistake. So will life as we know it. I hope we do better next time."

LARRY: As a lifelong fan, I always liked how he portrayed aliens. They were not always that bright, and they were always defeated eventually - but not before they destroyed ... well... a lot of stuff. For instance, in *Savior and Destroyer*, he finally has man solve the pollution problem, but at that very instant, aliens attack the planet. Or when we find out that the nuclear war was begun by aliens:

The quiet harsh cold; the landscape of Greenland. This part of the world had not yet felt the atomic wrath of the rest of the nations. A low humming breaks the silence, where the "meteor" had landed a sleek spacecraft now stands. Hardly of this world, its large tentacles like landing gear extended along with a large landing platform. From inside, two shadowy figures appear.

"Manipulate, you see," Androx rasps, "our missile was the spark needed to set this backward world afire."

"Yes, Captain. Primitive emotions were all that was needed."

"Once they destroy themselves we will take over and rule, adding it to our list of conquests," Androx said impatiently.

"Yes sir."

"Now prepare to take off, all we do now is wait," Androx moved his eight fingers along the panel, while his third eye checked the systems. A loud noise and flash of light, and the ship went back the way it came.

DAVENPORT: Once again, it's amazing how many things he predicted, not just sci-fi inventions, but sociologic things, how governments would be organized, even what ships would be named in our world and time. For a start: United Guild of Planets, much like the U.N. - even in their voting structure, the Supreme Assembly, The Council of Galactic Unification...

JENNINGS: And I agree - as a boy the names of the ships would spark my imagination. In fact it got me interested in history early on, as I looked up the origins of the ships names, like: Herclea, Lafayette, Valerie, Oneida, Norilsk, Ticonderoga, Argosy, Hatterras, Elektra, Saratoga. I could go on and on...

LARRY: And of course the Captain of Ticonderoga is named Ryne Torres. The Commander in Chief is named after Ryne's brother Mark.

Well... I wish we had more time. I want to thank our distinguished panel for taking the time to honor this sometimes forgotten influence. The question remains unanswered though: Why isn't Ryne Scott Paul Torres more well known? We know Orson Scott Card took his name from Ryne Scott Paul Torres. Yet the original is prone to obscurity.

One thing is certain, though. He leaves behind a great legacy. All that knew him or knew of his great work have been touched by his imagination like ripples on a great pond. Good night everyone.

◆ ◆ ◆

MOUNT ANTHSIA

KING OF LEGEND

The king swallowed and regained his countenance.

"You are a blasphemer! You dare to suggest that you converse with the Good One? Take him!" Before the guard could stop him, the wizard had snatched the tablet from the Monarch's hand and held it high above his own head.

"Let it be known that it was he who brought the curse upon you and that it was also he who kept the curse from being revealed," with that the wizard vanished in a cloud of red smoke... not to be seen again. At the spot where he once stood lay the tablet in four separate pieces.

The king stormed about the throne, telling everyone to get out. When he was alone he gathered up the pieces and commanded the royal blacksmiths to fashion a box that would hold each of the pieces. When the boxes were sealed the king sent for three messengers and ordered each to take a box.

One was to travel south, one west, and one east. The King would keep one to make sure no one ever again completed the entire great stone tablet.

When the king's messengers returned they were taken to the courtyard and killed, preventing anyone from knowing the whereabouts of the three boxes. After the king had sealed his box in a wall of the palace, the incident was long forgotten.

The king died many years later with the secret still locked in his heart.

WIZARD

The ancient withered hands reached for the tattered volume which had succumbed to another layer of dust and lay it open before his weary eyes.

The wizard drew his purple robes about him at the table. The room was lighted by flickering candles which, placed in animal skin, hung from the ceiling. The floor was earthen and had a wet, musty smell about it.

Wisps of dust cover the tome and got in his long, silky beard. As the dust swirled and stirred all about, he read again the passages which he told himself he should have memorized. The rest of the pages were torn away, but he could read the passage he was searching for...

"And there will be one who will come and make the separate parts whole again. For it is well known that as the four winds are scattered so are the Holy words. They are useless when read alone but will reveal the knowledge of the universal gods when complete."

Then further down the words read...

"Let him, the man, bear the mark of an innocent who is unjustly wronged and unwillingly pursued. For he shall need cunning and wit to escape his predators. He shall be as bright as the day and golden as the sun. But he shall speak humble with his thoughts. He will be man, prophet, soldier and boy. He will be a God."

The old man closed the volume and looked out to into the darkness of the street below. The starlight barely lit the dimmed walkways between the cottages, and the moon hung like a wicked smile in the western sky. Blowing out the candles one by one, he finished his long day by praying again as he had done these many years, to live to see this savior, this Good One. Extinguishing the candle by his large quilted bed, the old man rolled over and drifted to sleep.

Deep mountains he dreamed of. But in the early morning the man suddenly sat up. He'd had the dream again. As he lay back down, the mountain rumbled low and resonant and high above the sleepy city of Anthsia.

The old man arose, and opened another part of the volume. He skipped past maps, indexes, travel logs, flora and fauna, and the story of the other races that inhabited the underworld, after poem and narration, at last he found the page he wanted:

"The God now grew angry with Shiandar and punished it for its violence. For many weeks the gods of land and sea had windswept the county. Leaving havoc and destructive in their path. The very earth shook day and night. After ten days the shaking stopped. Shiandar it seemed, for a time at least, would be at peace. The foundations of the ruined castle shook, then settled back down for what would surely be another thousand years of peace."

Surely it would, he thought.

OLD KING DEFEATED

It had begun.

Shiandar knew well the ravages of war. One thousand years ago, far back into the dimly shadowed memory of its past, her people had stood on the brink of self-destruction and heard for the first time the pitiful cry of brother against brother.

In the twenty-third year of his reign, Axel the fifth, King of the northern mountains, found his forces beaten and driven back to his fortress on Mount Anthsia.

For two years his only son and heir, Brythan, had thirsted impatiently for the power that would have soon been his outright. His followers had engaged his father's other strongholds.

Now, with his army half starving, deserting and battle-weary, his best generals dead or missing, he himself pushed to the point of hopelessness, Axel grew weary, lax and incautious. By the time he'd learned of the treachery of certain trusted senior officers, he found himself being dragged by his own guards to be lowered over the battlements into the evil hands of his son.

YOUTH TAKES POWER

The battle was, of course, merciless. It was fierce and thorough. Many a good man died in the field that day.

And now all royal title and property were claimed by Axel the Younger. His first royal act was to hunt down subjects who were able and loyal to his father and execute them. With that done he finally could rest. Safe, that no one would seize power and overthrow him for the old king's sake. He was assured undeniable power over the realm.

When the day came to crown himself, the young king brought his father up from the dungeon wrapped in cheap cloth and bound in chains.

Placing the crown upon his own head, he proclaimed, "I am the one King!"

"With my uncles executed only this morning and most of your loyal subjects dead or imprisoned, I do not see much profit or use in your being alive, father."

With that, the new king leapt from the throne and drew his sword.

"Join your brothers," he said and thrust the blade into the old man's chest.

Even as he slipped in the blade, the old man was heard blessing his son and forgiving those who had brought his destruction.

NEW KING AND WIZARD

"There is a legend of the bones of 10,000 men. And a day in the foundation of the four kings. And now the ancient relic lives," a voice said from the crowd.

It was then, that during court that day, the dead king's wizard stepped forth from the crowd of visitors and noblemen.

"What is this, old one? You dare show your face here? Guards!" The King ordered.

As the soldiers surrounded him with lances leveled at his head, then the wizard spoke, "Hold I, and give to you, the secret of punishment."

"You mean the shaking of the earth? The wind and rain that befell us a week ago?" the young king said. From his throne, he continued, "my sky watchers tell me that it is punishment for your old ways."

Then everyone whispered as the old man pulled four stone tablets from the folds of his robe.

"Here, read it. See what you have brought upon yourself," demanded the wizard.

The king paused, but smiled, "Of course I'll read it," giving a secret signal to the guards to shut all doors.

He then sat down and after a few minutes turned very pale, "where did you..?" he began trembling, but then stopped in midsentence.

Everything began to tremble from high above.

The wizard spoke, "On the lofty slope of this holy mountain, the gods themselves gave it to me, reassembled by their hands, for everyone to see your evil heritage!"

Then, Mount Ansthia wept liquid fire.

◆ ◆ ◆

LOVE TRILOGY

DISCOVERING EACH OTHER

The first time I saw her, she was reading one of my stories. At least I sat there hoping it was one of mine, "It's you, isn't it?" I said, almost immediately, as if she or I even knew what I meant. Everyone turned to look at me. With all eyes upon us I moved closer to her. I'm sure she caught the eye of every guy. The type of girl who, when they hear a car horn, always smiles and turned to see who was honking at them.

As I waited in the restaurant for our first date, I sat waiting to be treated to a drink by tropical drums. Some place, I thought. It was half past seven and there she was, walking toward me from the cool night air.

I was tongue-tied and shy, she was the one to ask, "So who are you, really?' and said, "I need to find out more about you."

We both agreed getting there is half the fun.

I sat, gathering dust with the telephone. Sunlight trickled through a smeared window. The phone rang. I smiled and let it ring once more before I reached for it.

She was alive after all. While we talked, I could still feel my heart pound as if it were trying to escape.

It was so different with her. It was okay to talk about anything! I didn't apologize when I said, "Help me, I think I am falling in love with you."

She sat, eyes closed while the wind caressed her face, honey sweetened hair as warm air enveloped us.

I melted into her.

WITHIN LOVE

Enraptured. Beyond the rim of starlight, my love is wondering in twilight. There she was found in star-clustered reaches.

I had decided that she completes the tapestry.

In the quiet mood I saw my loving thoughts in soft retreat, receding. Her melancholy charms entice me. The slimness of the shutter, hushed. That she alone in my life offered the answer to my old questions: how empty must I be? How important were all of my past wanderings? She tells me it's a necessary struggle to find someone, to know its real, "Yes, " I told her, "I think you're probably right."

To me it seemed, at times, she was the very breath of life. I was just standing there and then she turned the corner as she took my arm and led me away from being alone. She was always smiling her smile that told me it was alright. Holding her head comfortably, but not in a careless way, she tried to use the moment to break the mood. We sat there. There would be a lot of that, in time. We had been singing in murmurs and whispers trying to figure out the entire picture.

I conjured stories of someone in a cape brandishing a sword in obvious regalia. Obstacles both real and imaginary come up in my stories, and for us.

"Wondering if they're right for each other," or "will there be a big revelation at the end?" As I spin my tales, we agreed it is a question of what people do in the present.

She gave me back poetry, the language of the senses. The slightest bit of long ago, to the present's heavy flow. We were at last in each other's arms, and for the rest of many nights. The whole of us became one, just like in my stories.

LOVE LOST

I ignored the games she made me want to play. I was swinging my bat but she wasn't pitchin'. As my spouse, she was not good to me in that other lifetime.

"I'll be better to you this time, I promise," she told me. Her voice sounding far away, yet full of trust and sincerity.

How tenderly we lie.

And then we thought, "well, okay. We've screwed this up, let's leave it alone." Despite that decision, I was still hurt and repentive three years later. Utter injustice. They say it's better to have loved and lost. Then why doesn't it feel like that? The memory of her was intensely with me the day I wrote this.

When we had lost all other recourses, when all other forms of enticement failed, we made a last ditch attempt at breaking each other's will. Thinking if we broke the mind, we'd break the spirit. I could see the destiny, the path: establish a process of her fall. I told her why the ring we wore has power. Maybe I didn't know why...

How tired we looked by the end, our eyes so exhausted. How tired we were of certain cheers and yells that had no life in them. Giving me no respite, no encouragement, then something happened in me. I don't really remember what. But it was the day before I left.

◆ ◆ ◆

THE FALL

Ryne Torres loved to run.

When Ryne ran he always pushed it to the limit. Since his junior year in high school he had learned to love getting up to run at six o'clock every morning.

One more, come on you can do it, he thought as he turned up his block and sprinted the last hundred yards to his home. Whenever he ran he liked to push it. He'd been pushing it since Olive street.

Today would be a good day.

He got home to the phone ringing. It had to be her.

"Hello?" he said brightly.

"Hi..." she responded darkly.

"What's wrong?" he asked.

"....Nothing..." That means there is, he sensed.

He knew.

"...I don't think you love me anymore," she said almost with a moan.

"Don't love you?" The words hit home as he remembered his doubt, "Oh Jesus," he said, "quit crying, what's really wrong?" he hated it when she cried and he was beginning to hate her.

"Can we do something tonight?" she asked.

"Sure, of course," he hesitated, " I'll call you later."

Damn it, I could've gone to a party with Marshall tonight, he thought.

He slammed the door with utter finality.

He needed another run.

~~~

The headlights hit him, then her car stopped beside him.

"Dorothy?" he asked.

"Get in," she smiled... but her eyes didn't smile.

"Just a moment," he thought of not going. He saw something in her eyes. But then, maybe not. He got in.

They drove. They rode in silence. Then he tried to be conversational but she didn't notice. There was something on her mind, he thought. Hell, there was always something on her mind.

She turned into a deserted parking lot. He looked at his watch. It was 10:45 P.M.

He had fifteen minutes.

The car rolled to a stop beneath an oak tree. She turned off the ignition. He leaned over and kissed her gently, brushing over her soft cheek.

Stars peeked through night's satin canvas as he looked at her, her hair glistening in the darkness of the car. A barely perceptible idea of an exquisitely shaped hand could be seen on the seat. She looked down, while occasional strands of blonde hair fell across her bright eyes and he could trace the outline of her soft, red lips.

The tiny lights of the dashboard danced upon her face, which seemed made of fine polished porcelain. She looked so fragile to him, yet she communicated a certain strength. The strength of restrained desire, as if held back like a tightly wound spring, lest it snap loose and reveal her true feelings.

He heard her breathing.

Now she turned towards him, eyes emblazoned and intense with expectation. They revealed the faint impression of a smile now. He sighed, as whispers of her perfume enveloped the air and traveled to the recesses of his wants. She shifted her body toward him, closer than before, her soft green eyes full of a young woman's anticipation.

"Should we stop?" he asked quietly, not sure if he wanted her to say no.

She didn't.

They were very, very close now. He touched her bare shoulders, then drew her up to his face. He could taste her.

"Ryne," she began to speak. Her voice, frightened yet commanding, floated between them.

"No," he said putting a finger to her lips, "no excuses or reasons. Just let it go."

Her fragrance blossomed for him as their lips touched and they became lost in one another. He could feel his senses become more alert as she pressed up to him. Slowly she drew him further and further down into her cloudy realm of loss and hope renewed, with each honey sweet kiss.

"I love you," he said.

"I love you," she repeated in a whisper, almost automatically.

"Look, I'm sorry about the past few days but you've got to..."

"Forget it... sweetheart." Then she just stopped.

"But..." he said, confused.

"C'mon, let's go. It's getting late, isn't it?" she said lightly.

He opened the door and got out, being careful not to let her know he was in a hurry. 10:58.

"Uh, okay, where are we... lock it?" he asked.

"No, it's okay," she said.

They began to walk arm in arm and he was about to say something when she stopped and turned. "Look! the tire's flat!"

"No it's not..." he said.

"Take a look, would you?" she said anyway.

"Dorothy, it's just a little low."

"Well look anyway please..." she said, insisting.

He walked back wondering why she was so insistent on? Oh well. He bent down looking at the air valve on the tire. He was not aware of the open trunk or of his girlfriend of fifteen months standing directly behind him.

The crowbar glistened in the moonlight, with its fine shiny coat of grease.

"Dorothy, I think that.. " he was stopped by the crowbar slamming down on the nape of his neck.

He crumpled beside the car and rolled onto his back.

He laughed automatically, "....blood," groggily he look up and saw her holding it above his forehead, "what?..." was all he could muster now.

She lifted it high, as he closed his eyes waiting for the inevitable blow.

She brought it down into his stomach, "Bastard!" she said, "I'll show you how to...!"

The pain began as a rumble in his stomach, then erupted. The muscles relaxed now, for a moment. He could feel the bruises begin.

He felt himself lifted... or maybe dragged? into the car and put in the back seat.

"C'mon baby," she said in a strange, sickly sweet voice, "let's go for a ride, sugar," she brushed the hair out of her eyes, "let me take where you like to have fun. Let's go to the beach. It's a nice night for making love."

The last words were snapped out like a brittle breeze.

His foot was dangling off the seat. She shoved it back, twisting it. He grunted.

She said, "You hurt? Don't worry, I have been hurt too. But you'll be better real soon," she finished putting the bundle of her mom's quilting over him.

Darkness enveloped him and it hung over his thoughts of being late. I am going to be in trouble he decided, as his body gave up and slid into unconsciousness.

~~~

I guess Ryne's not going to go, thought Marshall Jones. He opened the door quietly but he knew his mother had heard him.

"Hello? Is that you Marshall?" she asked in a sleepy voice.

"No, Mom, it's a burglar."

"Not funny," her warning voice said. A voice he had heard each day of his twenty years.

"Just going out for a while Mom," but she was already asleep. He locked the door and went to the party.

Marshall could already smell the alcohol when he entered the apartment building. The party was in a small apartment made up of a bedroom with a small kitchen and a living room with some battered furniture. People were squeezed in, hanging in and out of the kitchen.

His eyes fell upon her about the second time he looked over the room. Robin's face was still soft and inviting. A glow was still there, but it was multiplied.

She was even more beautiful than he had remembered.

But that chapter was done... for now.

Marshall left the party.

~~~

The car's headlights exploded into life. Dorothy Thompson put the car into third and tore across the wet parking lot. Leaves followed the speeding wheels. Darkness fell in behind then as the car peeled out toward a darkening horizon.

And the beach.

A quite stillness hung over the empty parking lot as the lights turned out automatically.

It was eleven o'clock. The wind rustled through dead leaves.

~~~

Marshall Jones was not in the habit of walking the streets late at night. But tonight there was something. His sister was visiting some ancient relative up north. He was worried about the end of school, work and all that. From time to time Robin drifted back and forth from things forgotten. He didn't know if just a walk would clear his head.

He was up to the corner of the high school. He headed toward the shopping center parking lot. A car was coming towards him. Saab '73, maybe '74. Good engine... gets cranky in third, though. It had to be Dorothy. That means Ryne's with her, he thought. Maybe we can go out for a coke or something.

He waved her down. She stopped and rolled down the window.

"Where you going?" Marshall asked.

"To, well... I am going to Ryne's place. We're going to the beach..."

"This late? Is something wrong?"

"No, I..." Something moved in the back seat, he thought. Oh, maybe it's nothing ...wait, by god it did it again.

"Well, I've got to go. I gotta to be home by 11:00," She started to move the car and almost took Marshalls arm with her as she accelerated too fast.

"Hey!" Marshall protested. Her rear lights slowly grew smaller. She didn't stop but proceeded on, and finally turned down some street further on.

Something's wrong. She was nervous, sweating, almost incoherent. Not herself.

And something had moved.

Oh well, she's probably afraid of getting in trouble. It's after 11:00 now.

He started walking home. The warm evening had dissolved in to a misty chill. He had to remember to mow the Peterson's lawn in the morning.

Something had moved.

He coughed and tried to remember if Mrs. Peterson had meant her lawn or the apartment complex's lawn that she and her husband owned...

Something had moved.

I am going to settle this right now, he thought, as he began to run home. I've got to call Ryne's house and see what's happening. And, what is the matter with Dorothy?

Less than five minutes later Marshall pulled out of his driveway and headed for... where?

Right, she had mentioned the beach. He stepped on the gas and headed for Ocean Avenue and the quickest way out of town. He'd do the ten miles to Surf Beach in one minute and then....

Then what do I do? He pushed it aside. He was good at that. Marshall concentrated and just drove.

~~~

Ryne's parents, Mr. and Mrs. Torres looked at each other from across the table when the policeman knocked. Mr. Torres answered the door.

"Sir, we've come," began the officer, "to ask about your son. A Marshall Jones called the station. May we come in?"

"Come in, " Mr. Torres said scratching his head and wishing it were morning. The door shut and the porch light blinked out.

Above, the clouds gathered, restless. Waiting.

~~~

Miles away, Marshall turned the last major curve towards Surf Beach, now just five more miles of flat, straight out road ahead. He turned the windshield wipers on. It had begun to drizzle.

~~~

Ryne didn't remember anything of the ride except, maybe... Dorothy's rambling about jealously and that occasion with Marley or something. An occasional burst of song.

Strange, strange, strange ...

"Damn it," he said as she rolled him out of the back seat. His head still throbbing, he was almost fully aware of where he was. The beach... dull now under a darkened sky. The sands on which he lay were full of rocks and grass, then it spilled off a few yards away to a jagged cliff and a swirling mass of rock and sea some fifty feet below.

Dorothy had gone around the other side of the car.

Ryne lifted himself up. He tried to stand but wavered and then again blinked in and out of perspective. The wind bit through him as he was trying to figure out why..

"Sweetheart," she said.

He turned and she stood before his trembling figure, the tire iron poised above her head, her hair blowing in the cool crisp salt air.

"Dorothy... quit... I..." he said, wincing at each word, "let's just..."

She let out a scream and rushed at him, "Quit? Quit? I'll never quit... bastard!"

The tire iron buried itself into Ryne. He fell trying to speak.

Suddenly she stopped, threw the iron down.

"Oh baby, I am so sorry, please... please forgive me. Let's make love. You can forget her. I'll help you..."

"Dorothy," he was losing it.

"I'll help you. Oh god you were beautiful... but now you've wasted it on some slut!" she screamed, returning to her former state.

She had the iron now, again, and swung it toward him, he tried to move but it wasn't soon enough.

Now the pain exploded through him. His brain seemed to burst. She was hitting, striking his already broken body... over and over now.

He felt a rib break and realized that his jaw was probably broken, crushed to one side.

He coughed up blood. His arm cracked as she swung the iron at his side, causing him to roll towards the....no...

Now he was dangling over the edge of the cliff. His good arm held onto some ice plant. He wasn't falling, but his grip became weaker. Blood poured from his head and his eye. His legs churned in the air. Even up here he could feel the spray of the ocean in his face... or was that blood?

He decided in that instant to live a few more years. The grip on the plants increased. He probably would have made it too, but for the tire iron coming down on his bloodied fingers.

The hand broke and he fell, hoping to die before he hit the rocks.

He did.

~~~

She didn't see the other car.

Marshall leaped from the car, ran across the wet sand and grabbed her around the waist. The iron whipped around and missed his face by a half an inch. He knew he only had a few seconds before she could compose her reflexes and strike again. The drizzle had become rain and her hair fell in wet strands to her shoulders.

The two police cars came to a muddy stop twenty feet away. The policeman started running for them. They saw Marshall and Dorothy struggling on the edge of the cliff.

And then she pushed him off.

The iron fell first, down and flipped into the sea.

"You're going with me!" he shouted as he lost his balance. Marshall grabbed for her other arm.

Holding her close, they fell towards death, swallowed up by the darkness and heavy mists.

His last split second of life he decided would be concentrated on Robin. Then he landed on the reef, breaking his back on the wet rocks. He tried to lift his head, but something snapped and he let go.

The drama was complete.

The only sound now was the crush of waves against the base of the cliff. The hollow wind blew between the officers standing above.

Lightning from ten miles out signaled the storm that had finally broken. It was one hell of a night to be out tonight.

~~~

It was two weeks later that a knock came at Mari's door. She didn't answer the door, because she was getting dressed for church.

"Mari!" her mother called, her voice cracking.

God, how I hate being hurried, she thought, buttoning her blouse.

"Mari, there's someone here to see you."

"Coming mother," she said going through the hall and to the door.

Her mother opened the door wider and Mari stopped cold, a shiver crawled up her spine.

Dorothy stood before her.

She smiled and thought how silly her reaction was. Mari, like everyone, was glad that Dorothy had only fallen to a ledge that horrible night. A few bruises, but that was all. Everyone was relieved.

Ryne had not been found though. Mari missed Ryne. They had become so close in the weeks before his death.

Dorothy told the officers how she had gone looking for him. Marshall had called Ryne's house and found out he wasn't there, then followed her out to the beach. There he tried to take advantage of her, but she had to protect herself. Marshall had a knife, she had said sobbing. Thank God she had the tire iron.

"Well, come in," Mari said.

"No, I'm sorry, I know you're on your way to church..."

"It's fine. Please, what's up?" Mari said.

"Well, I'd like to go with you and pray. I want to be friends... " she broke down crying.

"Excuse me," Mrs. Santori said, going to the kitchen.

Dorothy had dried her eyes quickly, "Can I go?"

"Of course. Mom, I am going with Dorothy. I'll get a ride back with her. I shouldn't be too late."

"Okay. Be careful, it's foggy out today," said Mrs. Santori.

"We will," her daughter said closing the door.

It was gray and thick as they walked toward Dorothy's car parked on the street.

"I am glad you accepted me," Dorothy said, "although..." she stopped.

"What?" Mari asked.

"Well," Dorothy began, opening the door, "I've been having trouble with the car's engine lately, but I doubt I'll have any real problems on the way."

"Oh," Mari said, getting in and locking the door.

"Do you know anything about cars?" Dorothy asked as she moved the car forward.

A moment later the car had disappeared around the corner. A stillness hung over the empty street. A strong breeze had begun to pick up and the trees began to sway, creaking and groaning under their own weight. The wind rustled between dead leaves.

◆ ◆ ◆

MARGUERITE

I shall be dead by morning.

So I will write hurriedly using shaking and unsteady hands, the tremors coursing through the very morrow of my bones.

It had been a strange happenstance of nature that I became a writer of horror and fantasy. Though no bright promise of literary greatness leapt from me in school, I had longed to tell a tale of dark doings and haunted houses for some time.

There were none of the standard macabre vignettes of childhood, no missing friends or sinister carnivals to warp my fertile and untainted mind. No, my communion came quite late in life by most standards, suddenly and with little regard for poetic anecdotes.

But it was real. Oh yes, quite real indeed.

Let me lay it all bare.

A shy breeze brushed across the tiny small green jut of land up ahead of them, coaxing smiles. This was to be a story of two people. A couple who moved to the Pacific Northwest from England. They bought an old hotel and begin to refurbish it. There was a cottage in the back of the property. It immediately becomes an obsession with both of them. They did not understand why.

They planned to make an exact copy of an English country home of this cottage. It becomes more of an obsession with her by the end.

The word Marguerite was found scratched into a floor board.

This story was to be told from the point of view of the young writer, a teacher of English literature who lives down the road. He fancied himself a sort of Nick from the 'Great Gatsby'.

He gets to do the research and finds out who Marguerite was. It was she that had owned the little cottage. Not a well known historical figure, but traceable. A story of a frustrated love affair, abandoned. Not conscious of why the new owner is motivated, the young writer continues to dig into the history of the cottage and of the elusive details of Marguerite. But the memories are buried deep.

Whatever lies deep in the human condition, posterity forces me to put all of this down. If for nothing else than to simply vent out my burdened mind and to keep my last hours sane.

As sane as they can be.

Three short weeks ago I had not quite looked all of my twenty five years. Now the face that stared back at me in the mirror was drawn and longs for rest.

I was a sickly pale yellow. The same yellow as the wallpaper in the cottage.

I needed no lofty explanation of ancient lore. Nor some mysterious house that had been buried there for a hundred years. In plain sight, but buried all the same.

I wanted the hell out. But it was too late for me, you see. I realize now that I'm not a good enough writer to tell this tale. The story of Marguerite has consumed me instead.

I can only offer a warning: When that sun sets on that town of yours, and things seem a bit off to you, just know this: In each of us lives the monster, the werewolf, the Marguerite if you will, masked by propriety and societal norms. If somehow or someday there came a release valve from the impending horror you see coming, let the lost tale be. Many things are supposed to be forgotten.

Run. Run like hell...

◆◆◆

TIME TO LAY DOWN

The air seemed to thicken with the heat. With each step the boy took, there was likely to be no reprieve from the summer sun.

On the dirt road that stretched out in front of him, a steady wind blew, tugging at his muscular frame. He scrutinized everything, from the tiny rocks at his feet, to the blue sky that appeared to roll on above him.

He lived in Duncan, in the smallest of towns in Central California, for six years now.

He still was not quite adjusted to the climate.

A wind, soft but steady, began to kick up dirt on the road ahead. He observed the tiny pieces of rock that he stepped on from time to time. Then, looking up, searched the sky for signs of life.

All around him birds chirped in the few trees that lined the rode to home. Bluebirds fed their young in nests made of dried twigs and mud from the now dry river bed. Edward hoped it would be full again by summer. He could remember swimming there when it had been swelling and racing with fresh clean mountain water before it began to absorb the water again.

That was so long ago now. She had long since moved away into the rustic two-story house across the valley. It had been just a few day before school was out, and suddenly now Edward found himself regressed in time.

It had been one boring day of classes just one short year ago.

No, he thought clearly.

Time to lay down the past.

Just enjoy today.

◆ ◆ ◆

BAD IDEA

"So, no one's lived there for years..." Larry began.

"Larry, who is this woman?" Scott asked.

"Legends say she's never seen in the day time," Larry remarked.

"I'm suspicious," Scott said, "that you didn't answer my question."

Larry avoided, "Hey, I am Irish, aren't I? Can't I be mysterious?"

"You're the photographer," Scott reminded, "you're supposed to make things clearer. It will be a sealed room?"

"Yeah, with all the instruments," Larry said, still not answering the question.

Scott said, "This is stupid."

"Hey, bud, probably nothing will happen," Larry said as he opened the door.

The equipment was definitely all here. All the photographic and recording equipment they needed to photograph a ghost. Scott sighed as he realized nothing was going to happen. Another wasted day and night.

A moment later mist seeped in and fills the room all around them.

She appeared. It was Anastasia, clad in white.

Larry dropped his camera and ran for the closet. She walked slowly towards the closet. She paused at the door. Scott heard Larry shuffle and move within. Scott waited, the breath in him all but gone. He thought she would walk through the door, but she simply vanished.

Larry started to pound on his side of the door. Then Scott heard a twisted gurgling sound, then a sound like muscles tearing. Finally, a snapping sound. This was followed by a loud heaving thud against the closet door.

Then silence.

She appeared again. As she went towards Scott, Anastasia smiled her white smile.

It was the last smile he saw.

◆ ◆ ◆

THE DEAD DOUBLE KISS

Two forces, then contact is made. One stays in the same place and the other goes off in entirely a different direction than was intended.

I am one of the "prime" people she talks to. "Remember I dream about you," she tells me, emphasis in the low breathy voice of hers. Speaking to no one else in the room as she walks by.

I feel disappointment when she tells me we won't be alone until later. She and Richard are going for a walk tonight, on the pier... perhaps.

I still wait by the door, half expecting her to notice.

Half wanting her not to.

When she does and our eyes meet, I do not look away. This is not difficult. What is difficult is trying to decipher what she is saying with those eyes of hers.

So, later we had dinner.

In my mind I imagine the accents here, very British.

"Hi Janet."

"Hi Ryne."

"We have to talk," she insists.

"Oh we do, do we?" I inquire.

"Yes, in some dark corner, preferably," she whispers quietly.

"Preferably," I agree carefully.

We walk past people chatting about this and that.

"Be careful, I have a weak heart," I remind her.

A glass of water is thrown in someone's face as we pass. She laughs at this.

"Here we are," she says.

"Not very dark," I say.

"Oh well," she decides.

"You were saying?" I started.

"I like your sense of humor and I think you have a great voice and I looking forward to working with you in our scene together," she confessed in one breath.

"Me too. But I wanted to impress you with my intelligence," I said.

She tells me she is learning how to waltz. It seems quite silly to me for she is so graceful already. I am enamored of the rhythm and the simple, gentle lilt of her walk. She proceeds to tell me of her previous interludes of love. Only most of them, mind you.

Of Michael, the 'quasi' boyfriend currently in, 'Gee, I don't know' status.

Of Frank, Naval Officer, good looking, smart, everything you could ask for in a man.

I am shifting lower and lower in my seat as I try to find the quickest way to run down State Street. She is baring her soul and I take some pride in the fact that she is comfortable with me. The more she talks of these gentlemen I become keenly aware that I am nothing like them.

By the way, just for reference, I put this down here, verbatim:

"So Richard is really dangerous," she confesses.

"In what way, Janet?" I ask.

"He's so sexy and charming," she replies.

"So you're afraid of how involved and intense you could become with him?" I offer.

"Yes," she looks right in my eyes, smiles slightly, "you're so aware of situations Ryne."

"Thanks," what the hell am I, her analyst?

"He's so cute..." turning away from me and staring out the windows.

I may be sick.

A little later, sitting in the booth, just below the air conditioner fan, from off in the corner I see our reflection. We look good together. Uh oh.

I do not know what to do. You see, I've never fancied myself a great seducer of women. As our love (insert question mark here) begins, I find myself occasionally baffled. The rain falls as we lie so close together. But I never really touch you. The house seemed empty without her there to hold. Often I would sit and stare at the bright oval of her face, frozen in the rendering of the moment. Why is it always good night, instead of good morning?

"Let's go on a picnic," she'll say one day.

"Sure, why not?" I say.

And we're off.

Eyes sparkle and laughter floats in the air around us on a sunny, lazy afternoon. Home from school, barbecue, family, safety, security, then raining, no rehearsal, just rest.

By the fireplace, warm, the first time she kissed me. She started on one side of my face. Kisses soft. I discover softness again. Then, before the night of the play, alone together. I turned and listened to the familiar screeching of the porch door. Her hand firmly pressed into mine, and she will not let me go.

Turn, please look at me, I think.

"Don't make me beg you," she says.

"Are you sure?" I ask.

"Yes," is all she said.

She was here after that for only a short, strange time.

I suppose this is the story that should have been written in the mature reflections of middle age.

But it happened just a few months ago.

A few days ago.

An hour ago.

I just left her.

She told me that she had someone and didn't.

I told her I didn't have anyone and did.

Slices of life, the small concrete moments and short stories in a character's life. Finding yourself, then finding someone to love you.

I guess it's time that I put it all down. It seems as I run out of pages in this journal of sorts, that it becomes less mine and more hers.

◆ ◆ ◆

POEMS

&

SONGS

DREAMING SWEET DREAMS

I remember coming home,
Dirt tired
Blanketed by fine soil.
I remember the mud caked between small, grimy fingers.
I was five,
Or was it four?
You know, you never really paid attention then because
There were kites to string...
Indians to fight...
And whooping and screaming and yelling and...
Dark.
7 o'clock at least.
Wars had been won and lost.
Mickey said he'd beat me up tomorrow at school
Did that girl down the street really like
Me?
The bath was taken,
Warm and soapy,
What a bother.
Finally, I lay beneath Walt Disney bedspreads.
Yes, perhaps I blinked once or twice, but
I wasn't sleepy or tired...
I wasn't sleep...
Soon I was dreaming sweet dreams.

◆ ◆ ◆

WONDER WHY

She asked me why I stay here
She asked me why I care
If she could only see herself

She might understand
The reasons waiting there

Just looking around I see them
Looking around I try
Turning around I feel them
But at times wonder why

◆◆◆

LAST SET

She had just started the last set
Closing time
Another single's Saturday night
Insecure hearts
Were setting up at the bar,
Getting ready to be knocked down again

I had decided to leave
About an hour before
But I just hadn't found the time.
I went in hoping I'd be there only
A minute or two
But my heart knew the crime.

Now that's just like me, I thought
Always waiting for the right exit line
But I found myself
Biding my time
That's when I caught her eye
And I knew there was more here
Than I could ever take again

She and I had once been quite an item
Made quite a pair
But the truth is

That doesn't matter
When you find
No honesty there

I wanted to say come with me
I wanted to say be mine
I wanted to tell her that
I missed her

Why had I let her go?
Oh that's right
Because all that
She wanted to know
Is if she sounded alright

So she posed in her love
As she posed in her art
No soul
No spirit in her voice
Or her heart

But the songs had taken hold

◆ ◆ ◆

THE REASONS WAITING THERE

Dressed so sharp
She cuts you
When she passes by
On the muddled streets of darkness
Past neon and
Wasted faces

I am walking faster
Than the law allows
Taking what comfort I can
In the light
In the night

Cloistered houses
Roll by me
And TVs flicker off
And on
A warm bluish glow

And all around they say
It's getting darker
But I can't see it
For the bright
Of the midnight sun

◆◆◆

IN LEAVING HOME - SONNET FOR LAURINE

In leaving home I return to something past
And finding long cherished lives unchanged
I search for some treasured nuance meant to last
Yet all about me souls become estranged
Through these clouded thoughts, twas you I sought;
Strength with a spirit guiding and aware
A peaceful shore sent to me in thought
A becalming breeze to soothe and take me there
Let not mere distance keep our souls apart
Nor hasten safe regret for absence sake
Though wandering still I've come to know thy heart
And from it cheer and comfort take
My sojourn having failed,
were you not meant
To be an inspiration
true and innocent

◆ ◆ ◆

ARMS AND WHISPERS

Look how still and attentive
You ask me if this feeling will last
If the smiles will fade
You taught me how to dance
So slow
We danced
And found we moved
So well together
Even the fast ones
Moved just as well
Then a pace slower
The music was there
Arms and the whispers in the dark
Hands slipped round each other

◆ ◆ ◆

FOR AMY (TIME ENOUGH FOR US)

My friends are all expecting another big romance
There's time enough, there's time enough for us
They're all in such a hurry
They don't believe in a second chance
There's time enough, there's time enough for us

I know I keep on writing words of Love
Afraid you'll go away
There's time enough, there's time enough for us
And though the feelings left unspoken
Can't be expressed in just one day
There's time enough, there's time enough for us

No empty signs and whispers
Just a quiet kiss goodnight
I don't need a look that's passionate
Just eyes that never lie

There's no need for explanations
No need to make things clear
There's time enough, there's time enough for us
I am not asking for a reason
I am just glad I found you here
There's time enough, there's time enough for us
Time enough, time enough for us

◆◆◆

I HAVE HER NOW

I have her now
After waiting for so long
Yet why does it seem
Easier when I didn't?

Perhaps that's where
Some strange truth lies
Is it always going to be true
That having something
Is not as enjoyable
As wanting it?

Now she walks my mind
Her graceful gait
The kind that bubbles
With that certain vitality
Does she still feel
The heightening of the senses
The way I do?

Why is it that
When I am around her
I am so afraid of losing her?

◆ ◆ ◆

I DREAMT A GIRL

I dreamt a girl.
She sat in a park
Young,
A flower just blooming.
Summertime
Had caressed her face,
Leaving its memory
In faint blue eyes.

♦♦♦

LAZY

Clouds march
In regimented rows
Like cotton candy in flight
Across a lazy sky
As I slept lazily

♦♦♦

THE EDGE

I came to the edge
I walked on dry hard ground
Caked and cracked
I cast my shadow on arid ground
While sunlight drenched my burdened back

There was no river now
Where once there would have been
Perhaps choked off
In the prime of life

Escaped for now from
That concrete zoo of steel and glass
Beyond where the wind whistles
With empty sparrow's song
Where love and compassion seem so out of place

The sun had found its zenith
While I had lost my own
And now I had come to this familiar place
Looking for the little boy in me

◆ ◆ ◆

LINDA

Be quiet my steps
When false words are thrown at your feet
To be discarded by the ones that utter them
Remember that I am true
That here you can rest
From weary battle
With the worlds ineptitudes and injustices
For my only want in life is to see you smile
The brightening of your face
Like sunrise on mountains
Veiled in morning mist
Like oceans cracking and thrusting corral
Onto the becalmed meadow

◆◆◆

SORRY SUBSTANCE

Oft times, in passions past
When in a state of muted melancholy
My mind's eye would conjure up an angel;
Some sweet savior in a woman's form.
And she would come to me,
Like some humbled lover's ghost,
Would haunt my days and soothe my aching emptiness.
All because I wanted it so much to be so

'Neath temperate skies,
near a romantic's own ruined shore,
It seemed for hours I could sit and compose
Sweet discourse, some clever verses
With which to woo my darling lady.
Though all these polished lines of love,
When neatly written and with dramatics properly excised
They only served the ears and the vanity.
Not the heart, nor the being for which they were created,
And were composed of a sorry substance.

♦♦♦

NO PERFECT RHYMES

You strike me
as one who needs
not the limit or confines
of structured lines
so unabashed and different
no perfect rhymes or proper verse
You deserve the unconventionality
of freer verse

For all my reason
all my rhyme
stops with you
oh, if only the words could flow
streamlined
true onto this page
no finely tuned line or
ponderous measure

You are here and so very different
my affection lies in these verses
no structured meter shall ever restrict what
I think, what I feel for you.

◆◆◆

LISA AGAIN

Here we are again
And we've both been here before
Only what are we trying to be this time?
Do we really want to hear the pretty words
We're looking for?
Are you ready
For the words I am looking for?
Lisa lighten up, again
The world can't be that much for you to take.
Feel like this and smile like that.
I want to hold you,
Bet that move would be
Much too hard to make;
Too much for you,
Too tough for me.
But I'd like to change your mind.
Don't be so sure the next time you hear a song,
It's not me that gently sings your name.
If we'd ever find the right time,
But it's always too late
For those who say it's so.

◆ ◆ ◆

SALLY ANN

Sally Ann
You're getting attention again
Yes, I think of you now and then
And I'd take the chance to dance with
Sally Ann

You were the one and it's true
Nobody could slow dance quite like you
On you played, broke some hearts too
And the music is playing
For another fine dark romance
Sally Ann

Listen, the songs haven't changed
And I've never quite been the same
Since the smoke got in our eyes
Sally Ann

From the boy who stood there
Though he didn't seem to care
He wanted you to know he's loving you
Loving you,
Sally Ann

◆ ◆ ◆

CITY'S CLIMAX

The din of the city rises to climax...
screech-slam-shout
the crying of the baby in apartment 4D
far below
the howling of cars
drowns the noise
of crowded sidewalks
windows bang shut
doors open tiredly
people push and scramble over one another
cars that lumber
down dank canyons
far into restless darkness
to get home...
all in one ebbing wave

◆ ◆ ◆

THE PROPER MOOD

Sunlight filters in...
Yellowing the blinds
I gather dust with the phone
Waiting for her
To call

I change as I learn
Don't we all?
About people, and...
I am just weary to my bones
So don't listen to what I say and oh...

To heck with writing poems

◆ ◆ ◆

A FOGGY SANDBURG

The fog sneaks in
On little rat feet.
It sits surveying
The metropolis
On nervous haunches
Then quietly settles in.

◆ ◆ ◆

MABEL

There once was a belly dancer named Mabel
Who slinked around on top of a table
Her reputation became failure
Because she was seen with some sailor
That's what you get for flaunting your navel

◆ ◆ ◆

YOU SAID I SAID

I said I'd never leave you
You said you didn't care

I said I'd always be there
You said it wasn't fair

I said hey! Let's get married
You said no, let's keep it cool!

I said look I really love you
You said, Oh, who are you?
Felt like a fool.

◆ ◆ ◆

LIFE'S DIRECTION

To be learned as Leonardo,
as mighty as Caesar.
But then again,
while others wish for greatness,
I decline.
If I had one wish, one desire, it would be
Tosurvivejustonemorecottonpickinday.
Because
Beyond that smoldering sunset might be...
Must be...
Someone...
Something for me..

◆ ◆ ◆

SHE WALTZES IN AND OUT

Darkness descends
You've slipped away somehow
Love it transcends
Wish I could find you now

Leaves turn
To the color of your hair
I've got to learn
Sometimes it's a crime to care

There's a girl walking rainbows in my dreams
I know how silly that seems
She waltzes in and out like spring
Now I see her face another place
And sure enough it's you

◆ ◆ ◆

FEELINGS PAST

One cannot deny
Their feelings past.
One can only
Surrender them
To memories,
Hold them,
Care for them.

Do not deny
These wants.
Once there,
Nor any love
Thy heart can bear

◆ ◆ ◆

WITH TEMPERED STRENGTH

With tempered strength of care and grace
Her loved ones she tends
Her angel hands can often trace
The cause of wounds she mends
An eloquent and wistful face
Where quiet thoughts contend
A Mother's heart... it knows it's place
Where love begins and ends

♦ ♦ ♦

LIKE A GLASS FIGURINE

A deer stands perfectly still
Reminds me of a fragile glass figurine
It's large, black, glistening eyes
Reflect the forest around him
Ears that seem almost transparent
Tiny nose to quivering tail
The fawn remains motionless
Like that glass figurine
On a dusty shelf
It stands in green
Deathly quiet
Listening for danger
The small slender body
Stands supported on
Toothpick thin legs
Three are planted solidly in new grass
One leg, though, is bent back
In anticipation of darting off

◆◆◆

TOO MUCH LEFT TO FEAR

Too old
For lullabies
Too sad and tired
For goodbyes
We lay
We lie
You sleep
I'll be near
When you wake
I'll be here
Too much
Left to fear

◆ ◆ ◆

SONG FOR JAN

BY RYNE S TORRES AND LARRY F TOMLINSON.

The things she needed from me
I didn't know how to give
We woke up together in the pre-dawn night
She said she couldn't go on living
What do you say to a person who can't find
A reason for the day?
Is it that bad baby, I asked her
Of course she just looked away
Every time she hurts that bad I said
The kids should leave
Their father could take them
Or maybe your mom...
I don't know...they just seem in the way
It took her a while until she could
Look me in the eye
You don't understand, do you honey?
They're my life to me

She was mad at me for a while
But the day went on and so did we
Her life would have to get better now
Because she knew she couldn't go away

I was a young man then
Sometimes I am a young man still
And other times when I think of her
I understand what's real
A true Love is a tough Love
It can keep some of us alive
But some never choose to see it
They just let it pass them by

◆◆◆

SOMETIMES

Sometimes
I'll see you
At night
While I am dreaming
Always there
With a soft gentle smile
Where did you run to?
Who did you fly to?
Leaving me sad
And alone
For awhile

♦♦♦

SHE'S IN LOVE

She's in Love
And she'll have you
She's in Love
No doubt in my mind
She's in Love
You've been hurting for so long
She's not in Love
So take it in kind

♦♦♦

LIKE A VISION SHE DANCES

The screen door slams
Mary's dress waves
Like a vision
She dances across the porch

She said
Let's move in together
Discover what is true
In me and in you

But she didn't know me
Or what I was about
She said she wanted me

But now she's leaving
And I am looking for some rest
Some space
Time to be myself

♦ ♦ ♦

NEVER THOUGHT TO SAVE

Now you and I go way back
We were something of an item
In our younger days
Remember the night you held me?
I asked to be taken and loved

There is a freedom I feel
In simply being near you
There is a freedom in
Being with one another

So here I am asking for time
Hoping to stay
Time was something
I never thought to save

◆◆◆

PROMISES

Grant one smile to me
That's enough to take my heart

With one playful thoughtful look
You add reason to my rhyme

Wish you could follow through
On the promises you start

◆ ◆ ◆

LULLABIES AND SOFTER LIES

Until you find the time...
Don't be so inviting
When you tell me no
Don't be so enticing
If you mean to go

If you don't want me
It's not fair
Knowing there you'll be
When I feel your touch
I could drift away and dream

That I am the only one
You hate to leave
I should walk away
Never tell you what I mean
So until I change my mind...

Lullaby's and softer lies
Will not still this heart of mine
There are no goodbyes
For you and I
No such thing as an end of time

◆ ◆ ◆

STILL

Still the songs are written
Still the songs are sung
Still the songs are written
The music lingers on

◆ ◆ ◆

SHE, REALIZED

She never looked at me,
As much as she looked through me.
I felt her.
I never touched her,
As much as I became her.
And all the dreams
I couldn't find within myself,
Well, she realized them.
The best reflection of myself
Shone through the passion
and the loving in her eyes.

◆ ◆ ◆

SOMEWHERE BETWEEN THE HERE AND THEN

His mind was full of her
His heart in need of her
But each step in thought of her
Led him away from himself
Somewhere between the here and then

His love
It ached for her
His soul
It longed for her
But each move
For want of her
He made in vain
For lack of her
Somewhere between the here and then

Where does it end?
This need
To begin again
Where does it go?
That feeling from lover to friend

And she was magical
A soul undeniable
And yet for the mystical spell
In her eyes, she was finally tangible
Somewhere between the here and then

And how he cried
No need to begin again
Where did she go?
Somewhere between the here and then

◆ ◆ ◆

GIVE MY MOUNTAINS A CHANCE

A city
full of harsh
disquieting sounds
The wilderness
can only offer solace
a sense of hurried ambition
in large metropolis
In country living
one can be himself
You work in large buildings
that block out the sun
Out here, in wide open spaces
time is your own
Why live in tall complexes
that squeeze you in
when you can sleep under the stars?
Some people can breathe pollution, not me
A city dark, grey and cold
I'll take clean air and blue sky
Give my mountains a chance
In this world there are different places
to be happy
all you need is
to find the one you want.

◆◆◆

WONDROUS MOMENT

Most of the images I have of her
Are beautiful and bright
Recalling them now sometimes
Gets me through the night
Life and laughter, smiling eyes
And light brown hair
Learning about love together
Not to really care
Where we went or what we did
We thought it would be forever
But forever is just a word we use
To describe a wondrous moment
We simply never want to lose

◆◆◆

FEARING NOT THE END

I didn't know what to say when
I walked up to her.
But I tapped her on the shoulder anyway.
The words I started saying almost made me choke
When her eyes looked into mine...
That day we started trying to be friends.
I knew it was hard for her you see
I was a gentleman .
And though life's strife will always be,
After a while the telling came easy.
The sex seemed to get better too...
We were both too afraid to think of being lonely,
It was something we could never do.
To hold her dear forever,
To never want to leave,
The laughter slowly sweeter,
Finding room to need.

I've always wanted you, dear,
Before we ever met.
The life and soul in your eyes,
May fate not soon forget.
Hopelessly romantic,
Of that I've been accused.
The nature and desperation
I've known seems so far removed.
From happiness and sweet caress ,
And finding in a friend,
Everything the world can be
Fearing not the end.

◆◆◆

ONE WEEK

You lover of words,
Now sing to me
And tell me of want and woe.
While all around us
Precious time slips past.

We know the days
Cannot be hushed and stilled.
Nor can even an hour slow to a stop
Sufficiently to sate us.

Take what time we can
'Till it moves no more.
And we like ornaments
Hang suspended in stilled moments.

Who would not take
What little happiness is offered us.
They could behold it
If only be for a moment's respite.

Yes, tell me of how much like heaven
A single instant can be,
And I will tell you
Of one week in paradise.

◆◆◆

MOODY VIBRATIONS

The orchestra resounds
On moody vibrations
It swells, mounts
Then sweeps over you
Like a wave on a lonely beach
Engulfing your mind
Body and soul
It draws you back
Twisting and turning
Deep into the corners
Of thought

◆ ◆ ◆

AFTER HER

Yes, he was after her
In a way
A way, he reminded himself
That was less exotic and melodramatic
Than her friends imagined.
He pursued, that much was true...
But it was the innocent pursuit
A child takes in capturing butterflies.
On we run
Jumping high in the summer glow
Grassy meadows
While that elusive
Fragile creature
Flutters through our fingers.
Once captured, how closely we scrutinize
Admire its beauty
Begin to feel more than just a little protective of it

We seek it as we seek any moment of respite
From this sometimes harsh reality.
Then, just when we decide to keep it
And put it away for safe keeping
On a pedestal
We seem to summon courage from the depths
And let it go.

If there was an attraction
As her friends would say
"Something going on"
Between them
He liked to think it went beyond
Mere physical bounds
She certainly was a beautiful young woman
An enticingly warm charm about her.
It went much further than that;
He admired her soul.

◆ ◆ ◆

EXPECTING TOO MUCH

Be sure to compliment her!
Men are not gods!
Women are not goddesses!
Love
Relationships
I expected too much
So no wonder I've been disappointed
Always changing
Acceptance of human quality
Mutual respect
She is learning this too
Switching into two modes
Is this good for you?
Organize
What are the next steps?
If you don't get involved you won't get hurt.
It certainly is the easy way out

I am angry, feelings are hurt
Not giving us a chance
If it doesn't work, throw it away?
Problem is solvable
Tell me to my face
If we'd met casually
I could just write her a letter

No
Done too much
Said too much
Well, if we ignore it
I want to talk to her
Her inner little girl!

Do you want to hear my
Side of the story?
We can't this
We can't that
Your body, your feelings?
My body and my feelings too!

◆ ◆ ◆

A KISS THAT NEVER WAS

I haven't given up on her, but...
If I could go back,
Retrace my life as it were.
To see her sitting there,
Expectant.

The kiss that never was,
Even though it could have been.
She said she didn't care.
I was hesitant.

Those lips were so inviting
Who do they belong to now?
Yes, I regret I never kissed her,
Softly...
Passionately...

I've befriended her
It's all I can do...
For now.
Yet, maybe in the back of her mind,
There swims a memory, a fleeting remembrance:

Of a someone who told her, "I love you".
A kiss that never was.

◆ ◆ ◆

HOPING, DREAMING AND WISHING

Shadows fall across the porch
When the sun forgets to shine
And in the growing stillness
I am another page in time

'Cause I've been
Hoping and dreaming and wishing
That you'd be the one on the phone.
There's no use in trying and crying
And dying to find a way
To bring you home.

Early in the morning hours
It's hard to make up my mind
Whether to break down and forget
Or go on with a love that's blind

◆◆◆

LONGING FOR ASPEN

You've been thinking lately
maybe Colorado's for me
no nicer place could there be

You're longing for Aspen trees
green and shady
somewhere to rest your feet
Colorado's for me

You've been thinking lately
no place would I rather be
meadows and mountains
and blue lakes and trees

Day after day you still try
snow covered peaks
in those daydreams you see
night after night you still cry

You know everyone says this place
can't hold her
makes her feel so blue
and every sunset brings her
that much closer
to someone that she once knew

Maybe a lover
maybe a friend
or maybe a little of each
like fire from heaven above
seeing her, wanting her
is the thing you can reach

You don't have Colorado
but at least you have love

♦ ♦ ♦

ROMANCING

Keeping to yourself, girl
Just ain't the way to live
Take it from me, girl
You've really got a lot to give

So hold my hand cause I'll want romancing
Maybe take a quiet drive along the shore
Maybe kick off our shoes, and get to dancing
Tonight it won't be like it was before

Remember those worst of times
Days before this crazy thing began
But sad never did look so good on you,
Stay with me and you won't be blue again

I am not saying it's gonna be all roses
I am not saying it'll be anything at all
It might prove to be a love not lasting
Then again, who's here now to break your fall?

There's nothing like a night filled with romancing
Can't get enough, need to have some more

◆ ◆ ◆

JUST A FRIEND

"I can't tell you how sorry I am,
I led you on.
He and I will probably last forever,
But your friendship will always be strong"

The empty nights of waiting are ended
There's no more fire in my heart
A silly love like mine can't be defended
She was only acting out a part

How can I be her friend?
When it's a lover that I want to be
Why do I play along? What's to gain?
I know I am nothing in her eyes, but
When I go away...
It's her I am gonna miss, just the same

Feeling like an unwanted child
A toy that's easy to break
You always played your bit so mild
Now it's much, too much for me to take

◆ ◆ ◆

IT'S YOU

She's blooming
Right along with spring
It's you
In the wind
A sweet fragrance that's deep
When the lights are dimmed
Wish I could go to sleep

◆ ◆ ◆

FORLORN

It's almost been a year
Since the night
That you had gone.
And though it's nice to know
You live
So close yet so far
I can't get used to
Living by myself and getting up
To an empty afternoon
The letter came late yesterday
I hope you'll be here soon.

Another month's gone by.
Oh, why do I try?
Why do you lie?
From day to day I cry
Seeing you pass,
Far down below
To torture my poor soul

Even though
I'd been rejected.
It's her I'll always want, always love,
I am sorry God.
No... I am sorry me.

◆◆◆

I JUST CAN'T GET WARM

Sitting alone in the quiet
Waiting for the late show
The phone's gathered more dust
Why you won't call, I don't know

I've been looking for a girl just like you
Shelter away from the storm
And if I don't see you, hear you
I just can't get warm

If you love somebody like I do
You have to get together, see things through
Want to hear your voice tonight
Telling me that we're alright
Have to touch your soul, tonight

Sitting alone in the darkness
Like it was a rainy day
Flowers have wilted
Just like they always say

If you could only see me
You'd know what it is to die
I love you now and forever
And, now you know why

♦♦♦

HER EYES LIGHT UP

The days were hot, the nights were long,
I thought I'd have to sing a song of loneliness.
She was there, but so was he,
By myself I failed to see, she loved him so.

And empty nights of hoping
That her mind was still on me.
Smiling faces lead me on,
Made me think I'd always be....

By her side and near her heart
So much in love, we'd never part.....

Her eyes light up when he walks by
She puts her arm around him.
I walk away, still smiling though,
To have loved her was a sin.

◆ ◆ ◆

TO SEE IT THROUGH

And we were, so you know
Not the kind to doddle
Will the things we wrote today
Still sound as good tomorrow?
Will we still be writing
In approaching years
Stifling yawn-some Sundays
As the weekends disappear?

We could stretch our legs if we've half the mind
But don't disturb if you hear us trying
To instigate the structure of another line or two
'Cause writing's lighting up
And I like life enough to see it through.

◆◆◆

MISSED CHANCES

It's too cold to walk.
May as well go to that dump I call home.
As I walk towards the park entrance, in the twilight
A face....
Only a glimpse, but a face.
It turns, I've seen it before. I know it.
Perhaps a link with the past?
Something to fill this empty life.
I follow her
Yes. Thank God for this chance.
She walks toward the heart of the park.
We can talk!
Alone, by ourselves.
It's been so long since I've communicated...
Wait! I've misjudged.
Heading for the bus stop
Run! Run!
Got to catch....
She's boarded
Wait please...
The bus engine drowns out the cry.
I fall to the earth, panting like a dog.
Dammit!
I live like a dog, no friends, no home
Why am I crying?

◆◆◆

A MESSAGE FROM THE GRAVE

You don't know how it feels.
For all your senses to cease,
Your limbs to be immobilized.
To not be able to move or touch,
In this world of cold and darkness.

You don't know how it feels.
Not to see....
To lose blessed sight forever.
To taste?
I can't remember.
To smell?
I've almost forgotten.
To hear and touch,
They're all so far away now.

You don't know how it feels.
There is a deathly cold,
There is quiet,
But too much of both.
Yet there are other disembodied spirits
To keep me company.
And centuries of misery and blood
Engulf me in a void of solitude.
You don't know how it feels....

♦♦♦

HOME MOVIES

Like home movies
Awkward
Novelties
A few dissolves
Here and there
Static shot
But fire there
Lots of fighting
For lack of better things to do
Let action move
But the shots are loose
No rule or precedent
Like a historical document
That's in and out of frame
This is enchanting
Freeze frame

◆ ◆ ◆

FEELINGS THOUGHT LOST

Pictures
of the girls he'd known,
or wished he'd known;
or should have known.
Take them out one by one
on the mantel
or by the bed
New inspirations,
old frustrations;
feelings and fears
he thought long dead
Seeing her again
he sipped a bit more
and knew he was well on his way
to being sauced;
the path to oblivion
with occasional stops
at boredom,
moodiness,
and temperamental moods

◆ ◆ ◆

A BREATH BETWEEN MOODS

A sigh and then a shudder
A breath between moods
So close
I feel the pulse of you
As you run through calmer veins
The simple quiet cadence of your step
The inspiration there again
Not begged or asked for
The words come tenderly and sure
As confident as your smile
Conscious of every movement
But denying them all the same

How many times have I struck out anew
Anxious to begin the journey again
The journey towards
You

◆ ◆ ◆

UNRELENTING EMBRACE

I would rather live with you
Amid the hush and hurry
Of troubled urgent lives
Than the hushed
Urgent grasp of worry

Be held alongside you
In time's unrelenting embrace
And face the subtle terror
Of not knowing what is to come
Than be alone in my fate

Complacent with the silence
A stilled night can bring
Accepting of a young man's
Brooding emptiness

◆ ◆ ◆

BACK IN MY ELEMENT

I had always been
More than just a little
In love with her
And it seemed that summer always
Heralded more eager changes in my life.
And just when I had begun to learn
The difference between falling in love
And simply loving
She wandered casually back into my life.
Everything I learned
Or was learning at the time
Went right out the window
Down the street
And far away
And I was back in my element

◆ ◆ ◆

FINDING THE COMPLIMENT

She still possessed balance
A sense of timing
Petite countenance
And still he was a good man
Or at least seemed to be so

He had wanted to be a writer
Wanting to explore the soul
She'd brought it out

We talk about
Being alone or independent
That we, each of us
Must be capable
Of existing without one another

And still we go on searching
For the other part of us
The compliment

◆◆◆

THOUGH HE HELD HER NOW

It washed over him
He had tried again and again
To write it all down
As if each word was going to
Purge him of her
Instead he wallowed in the hurt
It gave him to think of her
No answers
No guarantees

And though he held her now
Feeling her breath on his nape
And heard her whisper say
"I'm here and I'll never leave"
He could not know if it was real
Or something
He's written long ago
Left unrehearsed
And blank until now

◆ ◆ ◆

A HUNGER FOR CHRISTMAS

Away in the kitchen
To look for some beer
The turkey's half eaten,
We'll have it next year
The dressing is heaped
On some leftover bread
The gravy is molding
The peas taste like lead

Away in the kitchen
And morning is here
The cranberry sauce
Is still frozen I fear
My stomach is knotted
My head's in a vise
The food, no one wants it
Not even the mice

Away in the kitchen
There's nothing to try
Unless I risk death
And eat some mince pie
The fermenting fruitcake
Is something I dread
The ice cream is melting
I'm going to bed

◆ ◆ ◆

A SLENDER GRACE

Long, long ago
Into the stilled night
A spirit works for me
With loving eyes
With quiet hope
Staring patiently

With slender graces
And telling traces
She beckoned
With ceaseless longing
Until at last
The calmness of that night
Became a mere dissonant dawning

◆◆◆

WHAT WE WILL BECOME

To let not our passions consume us
Nor want simple absence to
Make a mockery of our true bonding
Lest the fire leave an empty shell
Where you and I once stood together
I stand here on the safe plain
While you tread deeper waters
Urging me
To leave more familiar dreams behind
What we are,
What we will become
And the temporary lack
Of your arms about me

◆◆◆

A RELATIONSHIP DEBATE

You throw something at me
From up there
Where you've made up your mind
Here it is
React to it
Let me know
What you think of my decision

Perfect relationships?
Who told who
"That's workable" or
"Nothing is final"
I have no time to wait
While you work it out

◆ ◆ ◆

ALL HAVE I FOUND IN YOU

I shall always have your touch
The feel of your body next to mine as we walk
Your laughter
Your loving, serene eyes
Inquisitive as they look at me
The breathy offer of your neck as we make love
A friend, confidant, lover and companion
These moments and more
All have I found in you

◆ ◆ ◆

INITIAL TRUST

She is full of great fear
The truth comes out
In actions
Seldom in just words
Initial trust comes
Not from the knowing
Or what is thought to be known
But from what is felt in the heart

◆ ◆ ◆

FOR WANT OF LOVE AGAIN

His thoughts wandered over blank sheets of paper
And from time to time they would settle
Lightly down upon them

His intent to convince her
It was just a momentary revelation
A mere glimpse of the true happiness
They could experience

This was his purpose
Together they could have
What they both needed
And would never be sad
For want of love again

♦ ♦ ♦

A CERTAIN FINALITY

There is a certain finality
In each goodbye we share
We touch for sake of touching
And try to memorize our closeness

Precious time slips around us
Why is there a silent "it cannot be, for now"
After each I love you?
Let us take good care, my love, and not sacrifice

Too much of ourselves, too much of our feeling
Towards someone else's well being
Remember to be true to us
And know you are my one true love.

◆ ◆ ◆

NO MORE TIME

No more songs are left for you
Written in the dead of night
No more time for you
To try and make us right.

◆ ◆ ◆

ON WE RUN

The stages we went through
Could I go back?
To the first poems I ever wrote you
And find that innocence and inspiration?

Did we actually gone through it all
Without you even having been here?
As the reality of the situation began to settle in
That I'd had you and lost you
In what seemed to be one breath

Just when we decided
To keep it and not put it away
We summed up our courage
From the depths
And let it go instead.

◆◆◆

A CERTAIN SLANT OF LIGHT

Where to start?
Where to begin?
How do you do that
When the story has already begun
Is still going on
And may never end.
Will never end.

◆ ◆ ◆

BITS OF BRILLIANCE

Like an unfinished novel
Fragments strewn about on white pages
Bits of brilliance every once in a while
But nothing to substantiate them
Now you're here

◆ ◆ ◆

JOSTLED ABOUT

Love without rationalization
That's what she said to me
One quiet evening at dinner
I looked up, half expecting to find
That teasing, curious sparkle in her eyes
The blush to her face
That would tell me of her jest
There was none

And in that moment we were truly met
Here, on love's rocky shores
Where pain and regret can be harbored
But a touch or a kiss to still lips
As gently against the fine sands of want

There should be no rules
No restraints or excuses
We sat and lashed out at life's cruel injustice
And wondered why can't we simply
Just love for love's true sake?

Wished, that by the very mention of the word
An incantation can be invoked
And the weary world
Would just fall aside
Exposing us in our truest, frailest and best form.
Should be, meant to be

We left that land of make - believe
Found ourselves lost in each other's eyes
Saw acceptance of how things are
Resolved to keep trying
And finished our meal

◆ ◆ ◆

SUNDAY NIGHT

I will talk to her
Look at the pictures
Propped up against
Some books on my desk
I can think of nothing else
But those few days in April
That fast approach me
Small increments of happiness
Are surely better than none at all

Everything does indeed
Stop
Afraid of rejection
We take the safe bet don't we?
But now she had convinced him of it all
He would not lose her

It was not only a face
That could never become too familiar to him
Words
Like a much too ardent lover
Can cling too much
Mine do.

◆◆◆

FEBRUARY 1984

Christina
Sweeter than a lullaby
Softer than a lover's sigh

Christina
Lying safe and warm beside me
Let your quiet charms entice me
Let your deepest dreams invite me...
And I'll carry you away

Carry you, to far and distant shores
Where we won't have to wait anymore
Now I've stolen you away
And it's here we're going to stay
I won't be leaving my Christina

Christina
Let my loving arms surround you
I am so glad I've finally found you
Don't you know by now that I'll be true
Don't you know by now that I am in love with you?

◆ ◆ ◆

THE HERE AND NOW

I have seen her standing
cold and resolute
against the grey, darkening sky.

Then I've marked her under softer light
where in gentleness and quiet we'd lie.

She reaches over a hand to me, a soft caress
the brush of lips sweet across my brow.

How often she invades my thoughts
between the here and now.

◆ ◆ ◆

IN THE QUIET TIME OF EVENING

You are ever constant, ever warm, never changing
The same sweetness of a lingering smile,
Secure in my thoughts of you
The always soft caress with which you trace
The contours of my face
That I could trace the contours of you
With just my mind but then, not only with my mind
For to feel the tremor of your heart beneath my hand
Would quicken mine own pulse
To race onward and know no earthly bounds
And when I look up and find you're not really here
There is that moment's doubt, that second of self-remorse
It is here in the quiet time of evening
That I think of you the most
All day the thought of you swept over me
In random rushes of intensity
Now, when the tumult of my passion has passed

◆◆◆

TO BEGIN

Is it too late to begin?
I look back
Down that long twisting ribbon
That has been my life this far
And can pick out the parts
Where I should have started

◆ ◆ ◆

RITES OF PASSAGE

Every time he has seen a man
Carry out violence or cruelty
Under the guise of being manly
It has ended in disaster
And nothing is solved

A boy comes of age in the old west
He learns that gentleness is not weakness
An outdoor dance
The rancher's daughter sees him
A boy learns that you can be a man
And be gentle at the same time

◆ ◆ ◆

TIME ENOUGH

Abandonment... yet not wild
Left alone with each other's quickened heartbeat
Alone to brood...
'Til our thoughts,
Like children at play,
Wandered to where they felt it safe
To hide and seek

No invitation to come along....
The wise and weary world quietly left us for awhile.
So we, ourselves more weary than wise,
Faced the unknown...
Unknowingly faced ourselves

I carried you away... to softer pastures.
The sunlight dances 'cross like down filled pillows
Through veiled shades of lace it shone, as you lay
'Neath cool shadows
And me.

Here, my thoughts sought sweet expression
And my passion begged your tender wiles
Eyes, green and clear, looked up at me... expectantly
The air, filled with our staccato breaths
Of fonder pleasures
Became warm and soothing, humbled by your fragrance.

This is where we stopped.
Yet it was not so much a stopping
As it was a beginning
A continuance... of what was before
And what will be again
Time enough for you and I. Time enough...

So we returned,
And greeted that wise and weary world
With an almost forgiving embrace...
While... outside,
The trees cast their dry rustled
Laugh at the fading sun
And we, long into the dark of the night,
Cried.

◆◆◆

REASONS ALONG THE WAY

Go... but not so far away
Leave... but not today
Stay... but not too close was all she'd ever say
Care... you know I do
Friend... that's all I want of you
Love... I can't think of you and I that way
Lost... in all the words we had to say
Lost... In the reasons met along the way

Days rush by
Nights drag on and on
Feelings die
But not my song

Care... well, you know I do
Friend... that's all I'll be to you
Love... that's something that flew away, and was
Lost... in all the words we had to say
Lost... in the reasons we met along the way

Too many reasons why
Talking but never face to face
Knowing there was something wrong
Now you've got your precious space
The only thing to be lost
And all I have is this song
◆ ◆ ◆

THE KIND OF GIRL

She looked like the
Kind of girl who was
Used to being stared at
But not seen
Used to not being
Looked at in the eyes
So I looked directly
Into those grey green eyes
And she met my gaze
Intently unwavering
In her own stare.

◆ ◆ ◆

IF I COULD FIND

In this dreary place, Ill-kept time
And find that I've replaced my love
lost it...

Somewhere between the you, the I and the we
I looked in other arms that could hold me
Or in a face that smiled for me

I looked... but always in vain
As if I could find a safe haven for my love
And keep it warm and intact
Lost, I forget how to love
Or wonder why love at all?

But even during all those times of disillusionment
I need only look at you
Your sweet face
Shining, as if the light
From a thousand stars reflected on it

For they may sing of blue eyes
But your eyes
Your green eyes
Sparkle with a brilliance that transcends any siren

◆◆◆

A PLACE TO REST AND KEEP

A question in her eyes
Answers in the touch
Awareness of the unspoken truths

Blue sighs
The quiet beating of hearts afraid to try
Soft light
Reflections of questions on her face
And there is a soul we search for
A hand to hold
And you and I may have at least found
A place to rest and to keep
With these dreams

So, for now
Take your comfort in sleep
Go on and sleep
While I just hold you
While I take my comfort here
And when you wake we'll go
And make these dreams we share
Come true

♦ ♦ ♦

SOMETHING MAKES ME STARE

Something I can't describe
the way you are, Cindy
Am I smiling because you said hello?
or is it just the fragrance in your hair
something makes me stare

Your lips, your eyes
make me realize....
I will always be waiting in the shadows
beside you, knowing that
I'll never hold you, console you, love you, kiss you
and when I am gone away
I am sure to be missing you

Then when I am back
and hear you say hello
it's easy for me to know
we're two different people
five different types of love
seen from above
But one kind of moment
one kind of love

Cindy, am I smiling just because you're near?
or is it the sweetness in my ear
whispers no one can hear

Cindy, you come to haunt my dreams
I can't be afraid to want you, to need you
but they're just cold dreams,
They are all that's left to me

So our paths will not meet
I'll not touch those lips so sweet
to be with someone I wish I'd never seen
for then this broken heart wouldn't be mine

◆ ◆ ◆

THE INTRICATE WEAVE

He'd been here looking for work for almost a month
It wasn't his fault
The relationship hadn't worked out
She was off somewhere to the north
With mom and with dad
It wasn't his fault the restaurant had fired him
Too much to think about

Where was the reasoning behind it all?
Every time he's almost made it
Every time he'd just gotten there
Tired and fed up with it all

Our lives are really very small
And tightly woven, aren't they?
The thousand and one strings of boredom
And placid monotony
Never seem to loosen
Even with the promise
Of real circumstances and honest interaction

Come down here, to this place, he said
Remove yourself from the safety
The almost sanctified embrace
Of a small town's quiet oppression
And you will have removed
The first knot in that intricate weave
You will have allowed the truest part
And sense of yourself
To begin shining through
A small light, yes, but what brilliance!
Honor can be a troublesome thing
But if one has it, one does not yield it lightly

♦ ♦ ♦

A WANT THAT NEVER DIES

I. Evening

In tenderness they glow,
The blue green fire of your eyes

The gentle ways of love
That only you and I know
A want that never dies

I always dream of seeing you
Bathed in evening's shade of blue
We kiss beneath a starry sky
And pledge our life anew

Caressed in quiet hush
Two souls slowly intertwine
I listen to your whisper
In a voice that's soft and lush

I am yours and you are mine

II. Midnight

Often I have closed my eyes to love
But you have set me free
Beside you...
When I need
When you need
The faint whisper of your love for me
A melody to make my heart sing
My kisses fall like rain upon your face
Open to the storms of love's soft fall
My heart beats
In quiet rhythm with my trembling hands
It stops
For a moment, for an instant
Then the night becomes fire

◆ ◆ ◆

MAGICAL LITTLE PARCELS OF TIME

He missed her
When she was not there
He longed to tell her so
It was this damnable
Waiting, waiting, waiting
Everybody has trouble with that
He told himself

The days were full of confidence now
Those magic little parcels of time
He would catch her looking at him
With just the right
Adjustment, at his head
And with the imperceptible
Tilt of her glance
He could quite easily
End up inches from her face
He could get lost in those brown eyes

He loved her, yet
Sometimes he could not express
The words
He had grown so tired of words lately
They felt so frail
When compared to the intensity
He knew was there
He would not try to fool himself though
To touch her or even hold her was
Constantly on his mind

◆ ◆ ◆

LOVING YOU

Night's fire long past
I wake with the promise of morning
And you
When day's unending clash and clatter
Seems to be its most unbearable
I drift back to the moments
I've spent beside you
And find solace
In the remembrance

♦ ♦ ♦

GOODBYE FOR NOW

The sun was at that wonderful slant
with which every face is given
the most gorgeous luster

She certainly didn't need it
That was the first thing he'd noticed
How certain light did more than simple justice
to her already pleasing features

♦ ♦ ♦

YOU WILL BE THE ONE

Familiar place
I've entered that door before
We've talked of other doors
You will be the one
To take me
To the rest of them
And walk thru them
And home

◆ ◆ ◆

WHEN YOU ASK

When you do
Ask me to marry you
Don't ask
After we've been drinking
After we've made love
Just before you are leaving to go somewhere
Not at venerable times
I don't trust them
Nor my judgment at these times
What we can do for each other?
What I can offer you?
What you can offer me
The time for customs
The time to think about it.

◆ ◆ ◆

BUT I AM NOT IN LOVE

I was raised to respect women
They are to be treated in special ways
Old fashioned values
Like my mother always said

She's right on time
But I am not in love
Because her pushing too much
Is the best example of
Who keeps settling for second best

She thinks of me as an oversight
But let me tell you
She finally got it right
I tell her once she noticed
That is why I left

◆◆◆

THE DINER

I sit at her table
Near closing time
In the dark
In quiet
Watch her earn some pay
And self respect
Her quiet dignity
Is dignity always quiet?

Smile
Never service without a smile
Tell them what they can have
And not have
Yet when she looks at me
She's not so sure
What she wants
What I want
Wonder if they might be
The same thing

◆ ◆ ◆

TAKE THE NIGHT

Fold up
Hit the dirt
Shake the sound
Of your own guns
Walk up
Take the night
Juggle your fate
And hold
It in your hands

◆ ◆ ◆

THE FEEL OF HOME

I lay in bed between warm sheets
And thick faded bedcovers
The dank air of my room
Listening to the sounds of morning
Bacon sputters and crackles
Its aroma invading my room
The eggs cracked and fall
Splunk splatter
Into the fry pan
That's brought out clanging from
Beside the stove
Cereal boxes are torn and pillaged
Doors open and shut
From acute cases of the grumps
And the toilet
Flushes and flushes and flushes

◆◆◆

SOMEDAY

Someday
I'll sit and write a poem
That follows certain rhythms
With no need to make decisions

I have so many rules
Yet even though
With life so set
And structured
The world
Begins to mold me

But my life
Is much too short
To follow
Certain rhymes

◆◆◆

A PASSION WILLED

The front door opens
She comes in quiet
As a whisper
A swept back passion
Willed

Dapple green eyes
Lilting and melodic
Search
Through older
More experienced eyes

She becomes clearer
I find her

◆ ◆ ◆

NOT READY

I am not ready for a big romance
But more than anything
I wanted to take her
In my arms, compel her
If for no other reason
Than she took my hand

How welcome her laugh had become
Her quiet stance
Unassuming yet full of subtle poise
Of rhyming praise
That sometimes closes in

No structured line
To keep her tethered
How intensely
And utterly final had been
The capture of my heart

◆◆◆

THE THIEF

Immediately
I ran after the car.
My legs moving
as fast as they could
on the wet pavement,
I threw my book after the car
(only thing I had at hand).
Hitting it on the trunk,
the brake lights lit up.
The car slowed and stopped.
The unknown thief
opened the passenger door
as I approached,
"Get in,"
said the sexy blonde.
My mouth slowly grinned.

◆◆◆

DON'T BE SO

Don't be so... every time you're near me
Don't be so... when you're feeling blue
Don't be so... when you hear me
Say that "damn, I'm in love with you."

Don't be so... when we go out walking
Don't be so... if you catch my stare
Don't be so... just let me know
How much you really care

Some people say this feeling isn't everlasting
Looking for qualities they'll never see
Wrong about forever, well that's for the asking
Forever never had a hold on me

Don't be so... when we are together
Don't be so... if you hold my hand
Don't be so... when you take me, take me slowly
I will understand

◆ ◆ ◆

MUSINGS OF LOVE

"I am confident," he said,
as he took her in his arms.
"About what?" she asked,
offering no restrictions
to his embrace.
He sensed this and was flushed;
boyish charm and giddy,
'where do I go from here?'
he wondered to himself.

"I will take you, kiss you,
spend this moment with you.
Will it make a difference?
I've always put such stock
in romance, in love,
relationships transient."

"I care for you," she said,
"but my past experiences
prevent me from
my standard naiveté about it;
not cynical, but...
quietly reserved."

◆◆◆

LIFE'S TOO SHORT

A world that's set
And structured so
Begins to bore me
Yet even though...

Someday I'll sit
And write a
Free verse
No need to make decisions

Because my life
Is much too short
To follow boring strife

◆◆◆

TAKE ME WHEN IT'S TIME TO GO

Until the moment that I met her
I was never one to take my time
Always thought I should be here and now
No one could make me want in
Would ever make me wait in line

Then I threw away those well worn lines
Somehow I lost a day or two
Because for all my honesty
There were feelings she already knew

And so there won't be any more goodbyes
At least not the forever kind
I'll take it easy and I'll take it slow
And she'll take me when it's time to go

◆ ◆ ◆

MY LOVE SONGS UP AND LEFT

My love songs up and left me
In the middle of the night
There's no more time or reason
For you to try and make me right

Should've been the first
Should've been the best
Should've known
That it'd go from better to worse

You tell me you've got a love now
But you're not sure it's the right kind
You're always there for him
He's always there for you

Not sure which way to approach
Take some objective advice
I am a gamblin' man

◆ ◆ ◆

HONEST EYES

Honest eyes
Not afraid to touch
Still there's a patient promise in your laugh

Anxious eyes
When we choose to look
But there is promise
In our patient words to one another

Shy smiles
Yet a subtle boldness to your touch
A young girl's sigh

With patient longing in your voice
And there is a life we dream
A love we hope for

◆ ◆ ◆

THESE DREAMS WE SHARE

There is a life we wish for
A love we hope will come
You and I are made of this
These dreams we share.

Quiet sighs
The quiet beating of hearts afraid to try
Soft light
Reflecting the contemplation
Of the questions on your face

And there is a soul we search for
A hand we seek to hold
You and I may have at least found
A place to rest and keep

♦♦♦

COMFORT

Take comfort in your sleep
And I'll take comfort in just holding you
And when you awaken,
For someday, wake you must
We'll go far away
and find these dreams we share
And make them come true.

◆◆◆

BUT TOWARD HEAVEN

A question in her eyes
Answers in her touch
Awareness of unspoken truths
Our feelings for one another
Found in such simplicity
A sound of promise in her
Honest eyes
Patient promises
When we choose to look
She and I are made of
These dreams
The distances between us fall away
They were once solid and harsh
Muted tones of grey and sadness
It used to be only in weariness
That I would look at you
See your face in all its half lit
Shades and expressions
By firelight, in dusky contemplation
Sparkling eyes shone by candlelight
An expectant gleam
And finally in daylight
Bright and ever shining
Looking upward, not away from me
But toward heaven and possibilities.

◆◆◆

WHERE

Here is where you should be
by my side

How is where you will be
in my heart

There will be a time
soon

When there will be a face
in the crowd

Why?
I am not one to look
like those pretty boys
who only stare

♦ ♦ ♦

VOICE AND PIANO

Mine is not the world of
Lost notes or words
That speak of my love
Stolen away
In some dusty pocket of my coat
Gone on some cloistered trip
Poet in the man?
Man in the poet?
No
Just a tired voice and an old piano

◆◆◆

PROLOGUE

It had been going on a long time.
of the infinite variations of solar systems
that could emerge from gaseous forms and clouds
they floated about on what seemed transparent tracks,
endlessly forming and reshaping.
The universe itself
never spared a moment's contemplation
In endless silence planets moved
across voids and chasms that stretched in every direction
as they always had.
Fiery suns, exploding stars, new galaxies
being born in seconds,
others vanishing in smoky obscurity.
Yet in all of this upheaval
a system rose majestically
on the edge of nothing,
took on a certain uniqueness
And in this system was a planet
that revolved around a fiery sentinel -
a sun which sat majestically
burning and spewing forth tongues of flame.
The bodies that surrounded the great fireball
swung in slow procession -
keeping time to a beat set long ago.
Most lacked the spark of life except one.
It was the third planet in the system
Not unaware of others of its kind in the system

it had given names to those others.
There was beauty on this one
unlike its brothers and sisters.
Green sloping valleys
gave way to rocky seas.
Blue skies that hung over
the journeys of birds and insects.
Mountain ranges capped in white.
Blue sky hung over quiet meadows.
There were green forests that surrounded
blue laughing water.
And over all of this,
one species rose to dominate over others.
They were kind, benevolent, merciful
but also hateful, war-torn, and self-destructive.
They had the greatest minds
and made the most beautiful structures.
But the people were confused.
The people made war.
There was hunger, starvation, death.
There were too many people.
As they began to explore the neighboring worlds,
they knew they were alone in the universe.
War was imminent,
as it had always been.
And so it was,
another planet awaited its destiny.

◆◆◆

REMEMBRANCE

When evening, dark and resonant, is not quite far away
When twilight's long cool shadow starts to fall,
Often do I see you there, in kind and blameless grace
And hear your voice in the lonesome night bird's call.

As dusk devours sunlight's last embrace
And daylight mourns its sudden loss of light,
Now fondly I recall when last we shared
What should have been a much more lingering night.

My loving thoughts, as if slumbering, recede.
Though calmer now, they n'er will forget,
That self-same fire, shining in thy noble eyes
As bright as mine, but twice as passionate.

◆ ◆ ◆

MY LADY

My lady spends her nights veiled
Beneath moonlight's silken lace
In unlit fields of heaven's grace
She dwells in darkened ebony sheen
Of wooded forests midnight green
Where ripples rush to water's edge

♦♦♦

ONE MORE GOODBYE

How many times will you play this song?
What right does love have
To be cruel and so wrong?
One more goodbye, one more goodbye

This boy won't do?
As if you didn't know, couldn't see
Why he would want you so
One more goodbye, one more goodbye

It's over now
The hurt will go to sleep
No broken hearts
No promises to keep
One more goodbye, one more goodbye

◆ ◆ ◆

OLD MAN

The old man sits motionless
Quietly on the bench
His gnarled sullen face
Like a wrinkled statue

Boys burst forth
Pedal past, peddle faster
Cavort and jump
In fluid motion
Screaming bloody murder

◆ ◆ ◆

WE'LL MAKE IT THROUGH

One touch
Kind and
So soft

Laugh
One path
One love
So true

Heart itch
Long past midday
We'll make it new
We'll make it through

Old souls
Have eyes
Warm nights
Glad smiles
Heartbreaks
Long past

We'll make it true
We made it through
Lullaby, colors of blue

Banish the tears
That are waiting
At the end, for you
Of the restless day
And I'll stay
With you

My words
Your tears
Our hope
Our fears
Hearts
Break

♦ ♦ ♦

MY MARBLED CAT

My marbled cat sits,
Assaulting dandelions on the lawn
Then, caught in a soft summer rain,
Stops and looks up, unbelieving,
As raindrops slide down her whiskers.

♦♦♦

AUTUMN

Autumn's golden luster
Was a shade off that afternoon
Where once I'd been able
To stretch out my arms
To see the rays of sunset
Wash over my skin
Turn it golden tan
But now what was it?
More than anything else
I was bright red

♦♦♦

LONG NIGHTS, STILLED

Reflecting on restless nights
Feelings I thought
Long since stilled
Many lines of clever verse
Would I compose for her
Yet something in those clever words
Made our love
Less true somehow
Hollow and then empty
Long nights, stilled

◆◆◆

HONESTLY FREE

The sum
Of a thousand strange circumstances
Never seem to come undone
Become an interdiction
To my journey of the heart
A sojourn to find what was lost
Gladly would I go again, if it meant
It wasn't just a moment's ornament
But was a journey's end

◆ ◆ ◆

SELF ANALYZED

Strength, weakness
Focus, focus
Relate to people
Relate to the situation
Work hard at change
Be patient and listen
If I'd been unwilling to compromise
I'd be them
But I am not
I want to be a parent
To be a gentle person
To just be myself

◆ ◆ ◆

CLUMSY CONSEQUENCES

I want to be remembered
In the thoughts of everyone who reads
There is nothing more challenging
Than a empty piece of paper staring me in the face
Pen to paper and all the clumsy consequences
Trying to get to the bare bones of the elements
Rain on my pillow...
Rust in my dreams
Got to clean that up!
I don't want to be around when I do that...
The things I shy away from now
Are the things I once thought true
One day I'll write that poem

◆◆◆

LOVE AT LAST SIGHT (I NEVER REALIZED...)

I'll conjure up a smile from time to time,
Cast a laugh at the darkest night
But the spell is always broken by the memory of you

You made me think it was so easy
So easy to be led astray
Now I wait forever in silence
Hoping you'll come back my way

And it was love at last sight
The moment I left your side
I knew I'd be wanting you, needing you
Now there's nowhere left to hide

So it was love at last sight
Though some know it from the start
I had to leave you there
To find you here, inside a lonely heart

Don't ask me to accept the way things are;
Just keep standing here and let you go.
When all you have to say is "come, take my hand"
Then I could tell you what you already know
I never realized you were the someone I'd be missing

◆ ◆ ◆

ALL I'D EVER WANTED

We're not without our share of thoughts or problems
And we're not without our share of lies
Maybe this is more than just a romance
Maybe not anything at all
But if true love isn't blind
Then I guess it's all been in my mind
Because you're all I ever wanted to see
You're all I'd ever wanted to be

◆ ◆ ◆

SOME LOVE'S FOOL

A little voice said
"Now there's a name
To be reckoned with."
You made it your own

Though you're familiar with my pretty honesty
They talk about that special brand of yours

I went on until you came along
I don't say yes, but you don't hear no
Don't make me an acquaintance
Of some love's fool

If I get impatient
If I sound confused
It's that too many lied
Too many rushed by
It went too fast

Oh hell, here I go again.

◆ ◆ ◆

ONLY SONS

Look at whose world we have ended up in.
what kind of life
have we tied ourselves to?

Remember the things we swore we'd do
whatever happened to the rebel in you?

And only sons were meant to make the grade;
put away your books and magazines
your paper pushing dreams.

Then hey, ok, the plans, the schemes;
now they're only burned out dreams.

We've played the game,
forgotten our own name
we've done our good deeds
now tell me, who does they need?

Only sons, only sons;
the best of lives mislaid,
tough guys aren't born, they're always made.

They tell us:
this is home and we should want to be there;
taking good care of the family plan
have to play daddy for a few years
have to grow up just as fast as we can.

Who's been pulling strings?
darkness closing in,
watch your back and mine
get ready for a fight.

We could leave this place tonight,
but we'll be home early enough.
another day of this life sentence.

They tell us it's not the place,
it's what's inside us.
who would have thought
we'd never see it through?

You couldn't have told us
sometimes dreams don't come true...

◆ ◆ ◆

COME WHAT MAY

No more carless lover's fond farewell
Just her being there to keep me safe and warm
And if there ever comes a night so dark
That she decided she needs the time away
I only hope she knows we'll be alright
And our love will still be waiting, come what may.

◆◆◆

PLAY YOUR SONG

Those simple tunes that felt so good
They would be strange yet familiar
A place that has no melody
A tune that's known to none
But still my song is written
Still my song is sung
And my love songs
The best friends I thought I had
How many times will you
Have to play your song
So then I won't sing alone

◆◆◆

THEN AND NOW

Now loneliness can find me
Back where I started from
A blue and quiet lazy morning
Perhaps you'll wander home
My lady back to stay
When will your true love arrive
Now and then
Then and now

◆ ◆ ◆

WINDOWS

If the eyes
Are the windows to our souls
Is it a two-way thing?
And if I can see you
Can you see me?
While I barely hold you
You see inside me

◆ ◆ ◆

THOSE LAST QUIET MOMENTS

While sitting
I think of your wistful looks and timid grace
how fondly I recall when last we shared
a lover's fondness, that deep embrace

How often do I think back upon
those last few quiet moments
we spent with one another
What could have been a former life
for now, that has to wait

And it's not enough just to say that I miss you
how do you make it look so easy
forever waiting in silence?

How I want, need, love you
for all my anxious honesty
though you knew it from the start
everything is all right
Now I want forever

◆ ◆ ◆

THE DREAM I WANT TO DREAM

If wishes come true
Then it's only because I am with you
And you're the only dream I want to dream
Feeling sorry for myself has lost its charm
How long have I been standing here
Wanting to tell you
How much you and I mean to me
Trying to act so tough and not sentimental
How long and lonely every night without you seems to be
So tell me, does our love make any sense?
Darling, please let me know
Don't tell me that it's just the way it is
Tell me if there's even half a chance
And I won't be letting you go

♦ ♦ ♦

EARLY
WRITINGS

FREE. PERIOD.

Bee, Bee Bumble And The Stingers
Mott The Hoople, Rachael Singers
Lonnie Mack And Twang And Eddie
Here's My Ring Were Going Steady
Take It Easy, Take Me To The Himalayas
House On Fire, Locomotion, Pocadation, Deep Purple
Satisfaction, Baby Baby, Gotta Gotty Get Me Get Me
Getting Hotty, Sandy's Cookin', Leslie Gore, Richie Valens
In The Story. Man, Vista, Fugiama, Kama Sutra,
Rama Rama, Richard Petty, Spector Berry,
Rogers Hart And Nilsson Harry,
Shimmy Shimmy, Co-Co Pops
Fats Is Back And Back On Top,
It's A Million Hits A Clickin',
Walters's Clock Is Always Ticken',
Friends And Romans Salutations,
Brenda Rends, Tabulation,
Carly Simon, Abby Road, The Rolling Stones, A Center
Fold, Johnny Cash, Peter, Peter, Paul And Mary Mary,
Doctor John The Nightly Tripper, Doris Day And
Jack The Ripper, Gotta Go So, Gotta Slow The Leader Up,
So Give Me Shoving, And Showing Miracles, Mushroom
Room With Bonnie Brown, The Wilson Pickett, Stop And
Kick It, I Can Get The Throttle Screamin', Hawker Jay
And Dale Amoni, Kukla Fran And Olie, Norman Oakland
Denver John, And Osmond Donny rockin' on.
♦♦♦

THE STALLED TRAIN

When my friend James Zachary and I saw the train sitting on the track we felt mischievous. We had just come out of Winchell's doughnut shop, and decided to inspect the motionless vehicle. An ominous sense of danger and foreboding came over us. Though at the same time, the rustic locomotive possessed a quality of childhood excitement. Having climbed into one of the cars we began to plot. Then all of a sudden the train began to move and pick up speed. James and I moved quickly to the open door. The wooden walls began to moan and creak as we jumped. The train was out of sight before we began to wipe the dirt off ourselves. I knew they were right when they said, "Never judge something by appearance, things aren't always what they seem."

◆ ◆ ◆

LIFE OBSERVATION

No matter how hard you try, there will always be someone who is displeased. Once you have corrected a mistake, they'll point out another flaw in the attempt.

As long as I've had friends, the need to be accepted has been vital. The emphasis we place on trying to satisfy standards of other people is not with parents, but with our peers. For instance, I can remember fellow students, with whom I associate, began to ignore me all of a sudden.

This situation had gone on for about a week when they approached me, giving hollow excuses for not talking. The whole episode finally came to a climax, and I was chastised for not talking to them! I simply related to them that I was doing what I thought they wanted. Their not being able to cope with my answer convinced me that there is no way to please some people.

On a broader scope everyone inadvertently tries to please everyone else. Society also sets certain measures. The way we dress is greatly influenced by others example. This seems to support my theory, because styles change and become out of date. Eventually people seek out another change in fashion, meaning that whole societies are never satisfied.

Never let your life be run by what other people think. It makes living, itself, that much easier.

◆ ◆ ◆

MY FUTURE

Last night I went home and sat in my room and thought. I closed my door and it quickly became cold very. You see, I think better in the cold for some reason. After reviewing my thoughts of the past day I write a little in my notebook.

Writing in my notebook is one of my favorite pastimes. Every day I put down ideas for stories or poems. From time to time, I write out little scenes or small chapters.

Some days I can write four or five pages of material, while other times the creative juices don't flow. I do all this because I want to be a writer. The courses I'm taking are all essential.

My number one pastime, though, is eating.

I really take pride in the fact that I can appreciate good food. Lately, this stomach of mine has been growing. So, maybe I should cut down.

I think I may be pregnant...

Moving right along....

I want to go right into college; most of my friends are waiting two or three years between. It's just that I want something to keep me going.

♦♦♦

GREATEST NIGHT

I was lost deep in thought: Somewhere between recognizing particle phrases and what year Iowa became a state, when a bolt of greased lightning zoomed around a corner and plowed into me. I never saw the kid that hit me, but soon a crowd had gathered to watch me gather up my scattered pieces of paper. Wondering what Mr. Arnerich would say when he saw Shakespeare speckled with mud, I picked up the rest of my belongings just as Schneider ran up.

Schneider was a tall, round-faced senior, and like myself, was constantly wondering how he could keep from growing up. He had a terrific desire to eat everything in sight. Nonetheless, he was a good friend in troubled times.

"Hey Ya!" he began "Watcha' Doin'?" Schneider was forever starting his conversations with "Hey Ya!" For two years my mother thought he had a speech impediment.

"Picking wet grass off of my wet book. What are you doing?" I answered.

"Getting ready for tonight!" Schneider said.

When I asked him why, he immediately began yelling something about my being raised in Siberia. He said that I had apparently become a recluse because tonight was the greatest night there was to be a kid!

Tonight was Halloween. I had forgotten.

Now it all came back to me: the candy, the hollering and yelling, letting the air out of people's tires, spraying paint on... ummm... or just innocently toilet papering an enemy's house...

"Meet me tonight down by the ditch," he said, as he smiled and instantly disappeared.

That night Schneider was waiting for me near the deep narrow ditch that ran behind my warmly-lit house. As we stood there mapping out our adventures I noticed the younger and smaller kids wandering about in costume. Little ghosts and goblins dressed in sheets and bath towels were scurrying around here and there.

It was about 8 o'clock when Schneider and I began that lonely walk up to the first house. It always seemed so foreboding. The door opened and suddenly laughter burst forth from the hallway.

"Look! High school kids, Edith! Come here and look... real high school kids!"

We had apparently picked the wrong house to begin our evening.

Two seconds later we were miles down the street. We decided to try again anyway. The second house was answered by the only drunk five-year-old I've ever seen in my life. After giving us the candy he kicked me and shot Schneider with a squirt gun.

Twenty minutes later, we stood breathing hard after having outrun the german shepherd that had loomed from the darkness after our fifth embarrassing house. The dog ripped my ghostly sheets in thirteen places.

I looked up and found that we were circled back now, approaching my street. I prayed for Thanksgiving to come early.

"Let's go," I said, and proceeded to help my broken, battered comrade down the sidewalk towards my house. We decided to stop first and see how much candy we had in our bags, because Schneider was getting hungry. Three hours of terror, agony, and sheer exhaustion had produced only a handful each of candy. There was also two sticks of gum and a paper clip.

Schneider began to sob. But he forced himself to stop when we noticed two small figures approaching us. I knew what he had in mind.

"Oh no, buddy, you don't need the candy. And I don't need it either. Let's just call it a night."

"No!" he said, "I am getting their candy and they won't be able to do anything about it!"

"Think first," I said, "they're little kids. They can't be more than five... Schneider."

It was no use. My friend was standing in front of them now and I couldn't hear anything but mumbling. Suddenly he straightened up and froze as the unmistakable click of a switchblade broke the silence. The two gremlins raced away as Schneider walked back slowly towards me empty handed.

"See you tomorrow at school I guess," he said, walking past me despairingly.

"Hey Ya," I replied and trudged home.

◆ ◆ ◆

GIRL FROM DOWN THE STREET

- Are you sure?

- Yes - look at me, this is not from over eating... are you ok?

- Great! I only look terrible. Well I'd better go in and tell my mother. Wait here.

- Mom?

- Yes, dear?

- Remember... remember how I was always asking about where babies come from?

- That was years ago, dear.

- I think I've finally figured it out...

- That's nice - put this plate away, son.

- I don't think you understand mom. I didn't buy a book or anything.

- You never were much of a reader...(thoughtful) just like your father. Come help me dry.

- You remember Kathy?

- From down the street? She's a nice girl. Too conservative for you though...

- You haven't seen her lately

- What?

- She's pregnant.

- That's too bad...who's the father?

- Me.

....

- Can you lend me some money for gas to drive her to the hospital? She says she's in labor.

♦♦♦

SOMETHING ELSE TO FIGHT OVER

The man sitting on the park bench took on the illusion of four children, with only one soda pop between them. All wore thin, ancient clothes that hung over their bodies a size too big. Three wore hats, covering the gray hair combed back like stiff wires. Each smiling, wrinkled face had a light hue of red in it. Like ripened fruit, the deeply furrowed hands wrapped around the other. Unkempt beards were continually scratched with dirty fingernails or callused hands. Childlike mumblings and grabbing for the bottle could be heard. They all talked with gravel in their voices. Occasionally one or two made a pouting sound and sat with chins buried in self-pity. All thought about how they were going to get home, on what had to be bean poles instead of legs. Soon the group had broken up, rubbing tired muscles as they shuffled away. In familiar forgetfulness they had left the half-empty bottle, looking for something else to fight over.

◆◆◆

MORAL DILEMMA

"Give me the keys to your house or I'll charge you with murder. I am the District Attorney, I can do it. If you don't give me $10,000 dollars I'll tell the feds about that shipment of heroine I saw you pick up at JFK. It's not true, but since I'm the D.A., they'll listen. I can tell you what you'll be doing for the next ten years or so, you'll be in Attica. Sleep with me or I'll tell your boss that you're under indictment for fraud. It's not true, but do you really think you'll be working next week?"

Sara Matlin worked there for eight years. She was the best, the most productive associate in her firm. She had clearly earned a partnership, but the only way she could get it was to have sex with a man who had the power to make or break her career.

Sara Matlin laid down on that couch for Mr. Talbert. What he did is called extortion and it's a felony. What would you do? Can any of us say that she really had a choice?

◆◆◆

MARCH 1976

I can remember feeling very tired that day.

I felt worn out for no apparent reason. Actually... this behavior had persisted for a period of weeks. Now, however, the affliction had become a more intense one, so my parents took me to the doctor.

The journey to the hospital was a short one. While colors and shadows swirled in and out of vision, familiar objects whizzed by outside. Looking out the window, I saw the sky was cloudless and seemed a translucent blue. Meanwhile the car itself felt as if it were a great ship rolling and pitching on a uneven sea.

Once at the hospital, I determinedly made my way towards the large antiseptic building. Inside, my parents lead me to a doctor, whereupon he told me to lay down. The walls of the examination room were adorned with intricate charts of the human body. I lost myself staring into out-of focus drawings while waiting...

I could hear voices around me, and they were saying something about me being a diabetic. The I.V. that the orderly stuck in a vein was hardly felt.

Mostly, I was too numb to feel anything.

Then there came a quick movement next to the table and suddenly I found myself careening down a corridor in a rolling bed. The attendant, who held the I.V. in clammy hands, breathed heavily as he tried to keep up. Lights flashed above me in perfect sequence until we entered the elevator. The doors slid closed...

I realized only later how close to death I had come. That's how I began my stay in the hospital, many years ago.

My new life began.

◆ ◆ ◆

WORLDS BEGUN

Until last year, summer vacations had grown dull and unimaginative for me. Those earlier Junes and Julys did not possess any flavor. They were boring cycles of orange Kool-Aid and potato chips, served on the patio....

I remember this past summer with amazing clarity though. It was like waking up to a whole new world after a long sleep. Places I'd heard of but never really considered presented themselves as exciting spots. This dreary town became electrified.

Suddenly there were things to do.

An old pastime of going to the movies was popular again towards the end of August. Mostly because of that cute blond who served the popcorn with a certain kind of sexiness. To come into the lobby after a movie and see her face, hot from working too close to the butter machine, was worth the two bucks.

The skating rink proved to be a haven for pretty young girls in town. On Saturday nights the rest of the boys and I would stand and stare as they glided by. Parties were common throughout this time also. Small get-togethers proved my new theories correct: there were actually people who knew I was alive.

As the beginning of school drew nearer the most important change in my awareness occurred.

Girls.

Girls were a formerly unfamiliar commodity with me, but not with my friends. Then after my sheltered veil was removed, I sought out someone to share problems and triumph. Even if I didn't succeed at that, at least I found a different life existed for me.

There were no more reasons to feel sorry for myself. It took just one summer to get rid of them.

◆ ◆ ◆

CLOSE ENCOUNTER

He could feel the wind tear at his beard as he edged the sleigh through the clouds. He banked towards the warmth of home. Santa Claus found life difficult on and around December twenty fifth. It never failed. After a quick shower, and some lukewarm Lipton onion soup, his nagging wife always pushed him out the door, shoving his enormous bag of toys in on top of him.

This happened every year without fail. Every Christmas Eve, Santa was buffeted between elves kicking him in the ankles and Mrs. Claus screaming. Making toys, hammering his hand instead of nails and getting glue in his beard was all he ever remembered of this time of year.

But, hey, it was a living.

Santa (his in-laws called him Kris Kringle) popped another "No-Doz" pill and hit the reins again.

"Hurry up, you dumb deer! I've had to go to the bathroom ever since we made Detroit."

That had been over four hours ago, but Santa knew he was booking towards home and would make it in record time. He was pretty agile for a guy of over five hundred years.

A loud humming noise broke the crisp silence of the frosty night.

A flying saucer came ripping out of the cosmos.

The large craft matched the speed of the gigantic sleigh as it swung in close to the eight reindeer. Lights blinked on and off as the hatch began to open.

Santa put a gloved hand to his forehead and groaned.

A small beige man stuck his head out. He was wearing a Harris & Frank double-knit suit, Thom McAn shoes and horned-rimmed glasses. The beige alien smiled.

Santa laughed so hard his eyes began to water.

"Hey! What are you laughing at?" said the tiny guy.

"You! I always thought you guys would be green."

"And I always thought you would be thinner!" Santa noticed that he spoke with a cosmic Southern drawl.

"Do you know who I am?" Santa asked after the awkward silence.

"Sure, you're the Easter Bunny."

"No, I'm Santa Claus, you idiot."

It was at this time that Dancer got nervous and began to speed up. This caused the rest of the deer to bunch up and fly erratically. Santa reached for something under the dashboard that he always kept hidden for such emergencies. He thwacked the panicky Dancer upside the head with the wooden two-by-four.

"Whoa, you moron elk! Whoa boy!"

"Hey Santa Bunny Guy, is this, uh... is this the normal way of transportation around here?" the little alien asked.

"No," said Santa, noticing the "STP" and "Go Navy" stickers on the spaceship.

"I am Santa Claus. I fly my sleigh and bring happiness, joy and good will to men. Then give wonderful toys to good little girls and boys."

The alien adjusted his glasses and looked at the huge guy with the frozen beard in the furry red suit.

"Sure. Sure you are, buddy," said the alien.

"Hey look, I've been out all night, and...." Santa began.

"Hey, don't get defensive Prima Dona," said the alien, "Oh, forget it... this planet isn't worth the trouble."

In one great motion he and his ship went speeding out and away to space. While this happened, the updraft at the height of 10,000 feet spun the sleigh out of control.

Santa regained control, but knew he had to land to calm the reindeer. The two-by-four wouldn't work this time. He landed near the town of Hogsworth, Iowa, population twenty one. Twenty two if you counted the midget bar-keep. Santa trudged into town. He had been approached by a police officer and tried to explain himself.

"Look I am telling you I am the real Santa Cla..."

"Sure, sure you are buddy," replied the cop.

Suddenly Santa remembered he still hadn't gone to the bathroom.

"Say officer, you have a bathroom in this jail of yours?"

"Of course."

Santa Claus hesitated no longer. He extended his hands to be cuffed.

"Take me, I'm yours."

◆ ◆ ◆

THE LAST MORSEL

There is an ominous silence before the bells ring. Here in the patio of the Lompoc Senior High, I await the deluge.

Now, it's finally rung, and the resulting scene resembles a day at Grand Central Station. Bodies wander in and out of the rustic doors of the cafeteria. They pass one another without uttering a word, but still a strange rumble of noise rises above the pushing multitude.

As in most crowds, small encounters do occur. Here and there old friends meet at the rapidly filling tables around me, while elsewhere new ones are found. The volume of noise grows...

"Hey, where are you going?" asks a forlorn friend.

"I don't know," replies the impatient comrade.

"Can I come?"

"Sure."

I figure out that the noise consists mostly of complaining about not enough salt on their popcorn. This, among countless other things, creates the atmosphere of pitiless starvation. Wrappers and paper bags are torn open to reveal the long-awaited food.

I decided to leave as the crowd settled into the usual routine of food-throwing and running about.

Dark ominous clouds appeared, brooding over the cafeteria. I didn't really take notice though, because I was too busy fighting my way past those tall lumbering seniors that continually stopped to comb their hair or glance in a window.

Being a freshman I had noticed that, more than others, my identity vanished at 11:35 as I joined that terrible surge of bodies headed for lunch each day. There, the reward for surviving those first four long unbearable classes came into being in the shape of a burrito and a malt.

Those great supreme judges who sat so high above had decided on something called a hot lunch program. I knew they meant well, but I also knew that they went *out* to lunch. So, miles away from where some superintendant sipped champagne and his secretary munched down on caviar, I sat with their compromise to a less than perfect system...

A small green apple, an egg sandwich, (I have a deep rooted fear of egg sandwiches, but when you're an underclassmen, it's 'end of the line, buddy!') a small carton of milk and a cup of coleslaw graced my table.

I searched frantically for a cake, potato chips or a cinnamon roll, Ahhh! to delve again into the deep recesses of a Hostess fruit pie! I closed my eyes and dreamed of the largest order of onion rings I could imagine. When I opened them, I saw that my spoon had sunk and almost vanished into the coleslaw, and the apple had rolled forty feet away through plastic wrappers and orange peels. The egg sandwich... well, my head began to sway, but I knew I could make it out of this purgatory if I could get past the massive bulk of the door monitor.

Then an idea...

With the chances and confusion of a food fight, I took my sandwich in hand, and let fly. I think it hit a huge hairy senior square at the nape of the neck. An only half-human cry resounded through the cafeteria and broke all the windows in the CB-3 building. Food of all shapes, sizes and smells careened across tables and whizzed overhead.

I managed to crawl and shove my way to the door and picked the last scraps of food off my shirt. The melee of stale bread, miniscule pieces of fruit and less than fresh vegetables was in full swing.

I smiled. The lunch program, new and innovative, had been a great success.

Minutes later the last fence had been climbed and I was bookin' towards some fast food restaurant. My mind full of greasy fries and oily tacos, not aware my watch had stopped. Lunch was over and I began running back to the first tardy bell.

Oh well, I wasn't hungry anyway.

◆ ◆ ◆

SURPRISES

I say
You're so beautiful
You're gorgeous
You're such an angel
I want you so much
You make me very happy
You're the prettiest girl
You drive me wild with desire
    I love you
        I love you
           I love you
You say
Um... I want to break up

◆ ◆ ◆

EPITOME OF FELINE

I lose myself in the stark white that
Curves around bright green ovals.
Dainty, the epitome of feline.
Whiskers radiate like fine thread,
Like spokes in a wheel.
From a tiny pink nose
The cat's tight little mouth
Is unusually still,
As it stares contented
From inside its strange definite frame.

◆◆◆

SHE LIVES TO BE

She lives to be
an effervescent burst of love and want
meant just for me!

Sacrificing, forgetting her own desires,
she serves me a slice of excitement.
along with helpful portions of compassion.

Wisps of golden hair fall across pale green eyes
that reflect the wisdom of the world.
all this, and she's only fifteen.
but then... so am I.

◆◆◆

LIFE SAVER

Despair is
Finding out it wasn't your turn to do the dishes.
Happiness is
Having enough free time to decide.
Love is
Giving her the last Life Saver when you know
You wanted it.

◆◆◆

TINY CRATERS

the lemon,
observed closely
seems to jump out -
attack the senses, fills the air
with fresh clean fragrance, the
outside skin almost smooth but
for tiny craters that cover its lunar
surface, secrete its own bitter liquid
from deep within, beneath the white
inner rind going all soft and spongy
envelops the fruit, the sections of
lemon surrounded by clear thin
sacks, yellow pulp composed
of thin strands. These leave
an acid taste when eaten
even through all this it
remains silent. If
only it could
talk

◆ ◆ ◆

EVOLUTION OF MAN?

Everything about the man
Reminded me of a large brawny ape
As he sat in the bus terminal
He seemed ready to snarl
The massive chest
Heaved up and down
Gave way to a stomach
That looked like he'd eaten
A ton of bananas
His hairy arms
Hung down from broad shoulders
Then his bus was leaving
He rose and lumbered across the floor
Towards the door
I imagined him in the jungle
Lugging that big hulk of a body
From place to place
With suitcase in tow
As he left I wondered
Does he have a gorilla's disposition too?

◆◆◆

EXTENSION OF MIND

Straight as an arrow, it rests
Cradled near my calloused thumb
Becoming an extension of my thoughts
As it flies across the paper
Shaped to a fine point,
Thoughts coming together, sharply
Writing words or moods
Able to topple nations
Or start new ones.
It's mightier than the sword, of course
And you can erase your mistakes....

◆ ◆ ◆

FROM A TO Z
Always
Beautiful
Constantly
Distracting
Ever
Flirting
Gee whiz
How
I
Just
Keep
Longing for
More than:
"Next time"
Or
"Perhaps not"
Quickly
Rendering a
Sweetly
Teasing
Unusually
Voluptuous,
Wink
X-cited
Yet not
Zealous

◆ ◆ ◆

MRS. FULLER'S TORMENTERS

Few people
Have any patience
With small rambunctious children
But Mrs. Fuller seems not to notice
Every day she faces terror
From eight to three

Crayons, pens and pencils
Begin to fly through the air
And she sits there
Quietly
Serenely
Calmly

Her third graders
Are the nosiest in the school
Though she says they're just
"Slightly overactive"

At lunchtime
Spilt milk
And crushed crackers
By afternoon
The watercolors and paint
Smeared on walls
(And other bodies)

When the last bell rings
Mrs. Fuller doesn't even jump
She stares at the cluttered desks
Now her tormentors are gone

She could babble insanely,
Or start to cry,
But she doesn't.
It's just not her style.

◆ ◆ ◆

JULY 10th, 1973

Today I am happy as can be
July the 10th of '73
Today's my birthday as you can see
Everything's all right with you and me

Thirteen years living on this earth
And I've loved it ever since birth
But with wars and hunger, filth and strife,
It's hard to live an easy life
With dirty air and dark despair
Killings and muggings and stealing and things
A lot of people just aren't aware

As I blow my candles out
I wonder what life is all about

I begin to think about what I hear
About this sick earth we have here
And I start to shake and tremble with fear
As I think, will I survive to see next year?
Yes I will.

◆ ◆ ◆

ICING

Lake
Emerald, Placid
Lapping, Flowing, Rippling
Like Icing On A Cake...

◆◆◆

USELESS

Hate
Slime, Bloated, Hairy
Uncontrolled, Twisted
Empty, Black, Depressing, Formless...
Nauseating.
Soured, Deadly
Loud, Sharp, Grating,
Tasteless.
Bloodshed, Broken, Crushed....
Hate Is Useless.

◆◆◆

SHOOT OUT

"You're a dead man!"
"Not yet I'm not!"
Marshall Jones grimaced.
The rock slipped in behind
and to the left of the ship,
catching the pilot off guard.
In the next split second it slammed
into his unprotected side
and ripped the fragile shell of the hull.
Marshall screamed.
It didn't matter however,
for in the next split second
he was gore -
blown into what seemed to be
a million particles of light.
A small silence hung in the air.
For a moment they were visibly shaken,
with a steady tone Marshall said,
"Let's play again."
The two Asteroids players dug deep
into their pockets for more change.

◆ ◆ ◆

Ryne as H. G. Wells

September 11th, 1980

CPSIA information can be obtained at www.ICGtesting.com
Printed in the USA
LVOW10s1045220813

349158LV00007B/127/P